Reparations
MIND

PHILIP WYETH

Also by this author:
Reparations USA
Reparations Core
Reparations Maze
Chasing the Best Days
Hot Ash and the Oasis Defect

Cover design by Philip Wyeth.

www.philipwyeth.com

CONTENTS

1. IN CRISIS

Several hours after the second Sentinels of Jubilee broadcast, HRA senior reparatician TJ Rowe tossed and turned in the bedroom of his Manhattan apartment.

David sat up in the dark and said, "Hey, what's wrong, guy?"

TJ brushed away the pillow that was covering his face. "I'm just really upset right now."

"You're overreacting. They'll catch those hackers. The HRA's gonna be fine."

"They're doing more than hurting us at work. They just humiliated a lot of innocent people. Including some of my friends."

TJ got up and put on his glasses. He took a pair of jeans off a chairback and started getting dressed. As he buttoned up his shirt, David said, "What are you doing?"

"I'm going out."

"At this hour? Want me to come with you?"

"No, David. Let me be, please."

TJ took the elevator down to the lobby and walked

out onto Spring Street. A cold wind was blowing so he flipped the collar of his pea coat up against his beard.

He walked quickly and turned down a narrow side street. A cluster of neon signs glowed brightly halfway down the block on the left side. He approached, but then began to pace back and forth outside.

Finally, he put his hands in his pockets and trotted up the steps of a storefront whose sign said, "Ming's Thai Assuage – Home of the Not Guilty Ending."

A bell jingled as the door closed behind him. A petite woman arose from a white wicker chair and glided across the darkened front room. She took TJ's hand and caressed it.

"Ooh, you shaking," she said.

"Yeah," TJ said, "it's been a rough day."

"You in the right place then. Mama Ming set you up with nice advocate. She give you good assuage, make you feel better."

"Yeah, that sounds real good."

"What kind of voice you like? Maybe high pitch like sweet princess?"

"No, no. Confident. Smooth."

"Oh, okay, haha! Lisa right girl for you."

The hostess went to the reception stand and started typing on a tablet screen. A door behind her clicked and she said, "Okay, room six. Go back, door on the right."

TJ eased down a dim hallway that had recessed red ceiling lights. Crimson lace hung in front of several closed doors that he passed. He reached room six and found the door ajar, so he pushed through the lace and entered.

"Have you been bad DNA?" a raspy voice cooed from the shadows.

"That's what they keep telling me."

A sultry Thai woman wearing a knee-length judge's

robe approached. She rubbed TJ's back.

"Hello, Debtor," she said. "No, it's not your fault. So many peoples before you did all that bad things. You are so nice."

"Do you think so? Can you help me?"

"Yes, Miss Lisa expert at assuage. Just tell her what wrong and I try to make the reproach stop for you."

TJ slumped to the floor. "I'm so worried right now. My friend, she's in trouble. I can't help feeling like we're responsible for letting her get hurt."

Lisa dragged a tall, heavy wooden chair next to him and climbed up onto it, then slipped a blindfold over her eyes.

"There, there, Mr. Debtor. Now tell me, this girl you know, she is Afrigro?"

"No, that's not it. She's a Cauc like me."

"Hmm. I'm confused. How you think we can make this stress go bye?"

"Just tell me it's not too late to help her. I know she's really far away from us right now, but I have to do something."

"You such nice man. Big. Strong. You do good each day. You honor the world…"

"Yes, yes…"

"You will help this friend because you must."

"Yeah, that's the spot. Right there."

"She your friend. So she smart too. You reach out brave hand, she know what to do. She take it. Then she heal."

"So it's not all on my shoulders?"

"No! Now we make it official. I, Miss Lisa, hereby acquit you of this weight of the world."

"You did it. I feel like a new man!"

"See?" the woman said, giggling as she removed the blindfold. "Lisa always work out the deep issue."

"Thank you. Now I know what to do."

The next morning, TJ took a water taxi across the river to Newark. Through his earpiece he listened to NPR reports about the nationwide fallout from the latest Sentinels video manifesto.

"We've had sporadic reports," a broadcaster said, "of small-scale gatherings and vandalism in a dozen cities across the country. Authorities say they have been able to step in and get things under control without major incident. So, considering that we have witnessed two brazen attempts to undermine the Historical Reparations Administration in the last week, the nation remains in an anxious but hopeful state of calm…"

TJ looked at his fellow commuters. No one seemed particularly agitated. Most were holding coffees or staring at their phones—but what were they watching? Sports highlights or embarrassing clips on the hacked HRA web page?

After the taxi docked, TJ walked the several hundred yards from the pier to the HRA shuttle bus while trying to suppress his nerves.

The scene outside the megabranch looked as if it could boil over at any moment. First, the employee door he normally passed through was locked and a sign posted on it instructed everyone to use the main entrance. Out front he saw two armed National Guard troops keeping a wary eye on the nearby crowds.

Some anti-HRA protesters holding signs were chanting in a circle between the long lines of Debtors and Beneficiaries waiting outside their separate entrances. A handful of HRA security guards also stood watch, and TJ saw one angry man get firmly escorted back into line.

Once inside the building, he passed through the

crowded Beneficiary lobby and took an employee elevator up to the second floor. He found half of his coworkers in tears. Some were sobbing while leaning into their computer screens—and most likely watching mortifying videos of themselves. Others were balled up in a group hug that grew sad new appendages as more people arrived for work.

TJ, freshly renewed after his late-night assuage session, stepped in and tried to cheer them up.

"Now, now, y'all," he said. "We've got to keep it together."

"Why should we?" one woman moaned from deep within the hug cluster.

"Yeah," a man on the floor wrapped around someone's leg said. "MARVIN's already been out of commission for days. And now this! How will we *ever* get back to work?"

This caused the whole blob to shudder and moan even more loudly. It slowly began to wriggle away down the hallway.

TJ watched it round a corner, then he stepped into his office. Jan was sitting on the edge of his desk. Her face said it all.

"Oh, Jan, don't tell me you're done for too?"

"No, TJ," she said. "Just really, really upset. And feeling pretty helpless. It's been a long time since I've been this low."

"May I?" TJ opened his arms wide.

"Of course, thank you."

Jan stood up and leaned into TJ's teddy bear hug. She wiped a tear out of the corner of her eye.

"We'll get it all back on track," he said. "Most of the people here have just never been tested before. They left college and immediately started working for the HRA. I bet if you and I show some strong leadership, we can help them calm down."

"I just don't know. But look, TJ. The real reason I'm in here is because I was looking out for when you scanned in."

"Of course. I'm touched you felt you could lean on me."

"I mean… Yes, without a doubt. But also, there's an FBI investigator in the conference room right now. And he wants to talk to you."

"Me? What on earth for?"

"I don't have the faintest idea. But this all got really serious as of last night. I've got a hundred things to do that are all marked urgent. So I've got to go. Do your best in there. I'll catch up with you maybe later in the afternoon."

"Okay, boss. Chin up."

"Thank you."

TJ began to walk toward the conference room. An icy chill was in the air. Ever since that first hack which undermined confidence in the HRA, it had been a struggle for the employees to believe that things would be okay—let alone put on a good face for the upset citizens downstairs or calling in on video chat. Now their anxiety had turned into near panic.

TJ had seen this shocked desperation firsthand as a child and again as a teenager, when the 2000 dot-com and 2008 Wall Street crashes chopped his parents and friends' families off at the knees. But being resilient Southerners, they'd battled through and rebuilt their lives stoically. TJ carried with him this dust-yourself-off attitude, even after moving far away and later joining the vanguard of a political movement that was vastly different from his family's politics. He may have been the outlier, but at his core their pragmatic values remained.

TJ was annoyed that the FBI wanted to interview him at a time when he felt he should be rallying his team. So he went into the kitchen and prepared a cup of coffee as slowly as possible, fully stirring in each packet of sugar before adding another. He also used the restroom before finally reaching the conference room, where a middle-aged man in a shimmering black suit was waiting with a stack of folders and two tablets laid out.

"Ah, Mr. Rowe," the man said. "Nice to see you at last. Please have a seat."

"And you are?"

"Agent Wynn. FBI special investigations. I'm on the national task force that's trying to figure out what the hell is going on with these hacks. And after last night's business, we've got no time to waste."

"I'm here."

"Now, TJ. I see that you're one of the lead reparaticians at this branch. Would it be safe to say that you know a lot of what goes on around here?"

"Within reason. You think I might be able to help catch the hackers?"

"Uh, not exactly. I called you in here privately because your name actually came up."

"*My* name? For what?"

"I don't quite know. It's just that your name came up and I'd like to give you a chance to explain yourself. You know, tell your side."

"Tell my side of what?"

Agent Wynn opened a folder and started flipping through the pages.

"All I know is that someone thinks you might be one of the moles that the Sentinels planted. Now, I don't know if that's true, and we're not running a kangaroo court here. So let's just chat."

"Listen, I'm a technician. What interests me are microfibers and using my expertise to toss out forgeries that might undermine the HRA's effectiveness. If I was working for the other side, I could just falsify documents on my own to cause problems. Do you have any evidence to suspect me of doing that?"

"Now, now. Don't get curt with me. I'm just doing my job. Something's wrong here at the HRA and they called in the pros to straighten things out."

TJ sat back and crossed his arms. "Oh, I get it now. We're the new kid in town so the big boys think they can drop in to get us to heel."

"Call it respect for your elders."

"Sir, let me tell you something. I'm as progressive as they come, but I *am* from the South. We remember Waco and that fishy business out in Oklahoma City— so don't look at me like some pushover sitting in awe of you guys at the FBI."

"You want to make me the bad guy? I've got the power here, bub. The power to clear your name so you can get back to fiddling with your ancient scrolls. And the power to haul you in to my district office and play hardball. Because this is no laughing matter! You wanna get cute with me about thirty-year-old cases? There's trillions of dollars on the line right now!

"I'm talking about the credibility of the US government, and respect for the office of the president! This goes way beyond party lines, ideology, even belief in Reparations itself. And yet you sit there smug, just like you have since the day of the first hack. Yeah, I know about you and your cavalier attitude. And still you wonder why I've got you in here."

TJ put his palms on the table. "I've simply been trying to keep my cool while everyone else got weak at the knees. Setbacks happen!"

"You know," Wynn said, "having a hard drive crash is a setback. But someone hacking into the mainframe of your whole operation is a bit of a bigger deal, wouldn't you say? I'd like nothing more than to cross your name off my list so I don't waste any more time on a dead end. What do you say, can you work with me here?"

"Okay. Now that we're square."

"Tell me, then. Did you know anything about the hack beforehand?"

"Of course not."

Agent Wynn looked down at his papers.

"Have you ever been in contact with, or provided internal data to, any person you know to be a member of the Sentinels of Jubilee?"

"I told you, no. And you'll get that same answer from me all day."

"Noted. Alright, go run on back to your documents. But don't forget, I've got my eye on you."

TJ left without saying another word and stomped back into his office. He left the door open and spent the next hour collating a stack of old contracts that were backlogged because MARVIN remained in lockdown.

He briefly consulted with several of his assistants, then took the elevator to the ground level and left the building. He ignored the crowds outside and walked to a sandwich shop a few blocks away, ordering lunch to go.

With paper bag in hand he walked toward a nearby park, but ordered a taxi with his phone so that just as he reached a picnic table, he was able to quickly duck into the back seat of an approaching car.

A mile down the road he asked to be let out.

"But it says you want to go across river," the driver barked. "Come on, man! I thought I was getting nice fare!"

"Sorry. Here's lunch instead."

TJ dropped the paper bag onto the front passenger seat and got out of the cab. He heard the driver mutter something in Russian as he shut the door and walked away.

He turned down a side alley and dialed his phone. His coworker and friend Kate Donohugh answered.

"Oh my God! TJ! I'm so glad to hear from you."

"And do we ever need to talk. But first off, how are you? *Where* are you now?"

"Still in South Dakota, unfortunately. They kept me here at the hospital overnight. Luis is still unconscious. I don't know what's going on or what they expect me to do."

"Things aren't any better back here either. It's crazy outside the office. And some suit just pulled me into an interrogation—as if *I* was one of the spies!"

"Please tell me that you're not. I just couldn't handle it."

"Hell no, I'm not in on the hack. Jesus! But that's not the only reason why I'm calling. Kate, as bad as that ordeal was, I've been feeling just awful for you."

"Thank you, TJ. I mean it."

"That they would specifically target you because you were on *DDM TV* during their first hack. And then to use that footage of you when you were at your weakest—disgusting."

"I couldn't even take Chris's call after it happened. I cried all night in this patient room they stuck me in."

"I'm so sorry. Now things are really getting nasty. Seems like everyone's swarming around us."

"It's sad but true," Kate sighed. "The best I could come up with to calm myself down this morning was knowing that they've got footage of everyone. It was just the worst possible luck that my life played into their narrative. For two weeks I was already the poster child for the HRA and that TV show—the Sentinels just took the baton and kept running with it."

"God, I admire your strength. Because honestly, I was so upset thinking about how we let you get dragged into everyone's nets without our support."

"Don't say that, TJ. I know you all care about me."

"We really do. Did you end up talking to Chris?"

"I finally called him a little while ago. He's just as mad as you are. He says I've given more than enough to everybody. Wants to take a vacation so we can clear our heads."

"So do it! It's been a hell of a year for you, take a break."

"I know, I know. It's just—for some reason I can't face him right now. There's this new feeling of doubt in the back of my mind that I need to understand. I mean, how did it all end up here like this? How did my life—which I spent doing everything to help others from the bottom of my heart—how did that turn into me becoming the object of ridicule in the middle of a political disaster? Not only is my whole life's work possibly falling apart, but some people are saying we're on the verge of a second civil war!"

"You can't put it all on yourself. You're just one of thousands of cogs in this machine that's behind Reparations."

"But that's exactly it. We're all willing cogs. We signed up for it. Like that famous line, 'We hold these truths to be self-evident,' and therefore we must do X. But I don't remember ever debating the merits and defects of what we believe. I mean, I always *thought* I was my own person, but now I wonder if there's some narrative or script that I've been going off the whole time."

"So, what? You don't think the Kate that I know and care about is the real you? 'Cause if that's the case, what can you even do to find her?"

"I feel like somehow I have to go to the source. Not to find out 'where it all went wrong,' but to know how I found myself on this path. Because what if I was just *put* on it, and there was never a fork in the road or a series of truly different options? Then every choice was just an illusion, and in the end we all got funneled to serve their agenda."

"And who are they?" TJ asked.

"I know, that's the trillion-dollar question. First asked by every tin-foil-hat-wearing conspiracy guy. And now by obedient little Kate Donohugh, the woman who dedicated her life to caring about the world. But I have to know, has somebody really been pulling my strings?"

"Kate, just be really careful going down that rabbit hole. Sometimes the person who comes back is so shook up by the new knowledge, that it would probably have been better to stay in the dark."

"I hear you. Any other time and I wouldn't go there. But this year I've been dragged through a lot of drama. I can't face the next forty years of my life blindly going off assumptions anymore. I've got to put the old me to the test and see who's really left standing afterwards. And... I think I have to do it alone."

"Then trust your gut. And don't be in any rush to come back here. People are so paranoid right now that this could turn into a witch-hunt. Or if the public loses confidence in the program... Who knows how bad things could get?"

"Good God."

"The National Guard was already out there this

morning. Seriously, *do not* come back unless they force you to."

"But won't that also make me look suspicious? Am I just supposed to sit around my apartment while you're across the water dealing with all this stress?"

"I don't have the answers. All I know is that everything we've worked for is in jeopardy. Kate, I don't want our legacy to be that we only got in three good years before it all fell apart."

"I know! Somehow we've got to reestablish morale within our ranks. But how do you rebuild the trust when there could be a mole sitting right next to you?"

"This is like some episode of the *Twilight Zone*. Friends and allies turning against each other."

Kate paused. "Hey, TJ? I've got to get off the phone now. Something's going on and they need me."

"Okay. Just remember, you're the good guy here. Don't let them intimidate you."

"Goodbye, buddy…"

Kate set her phone down and turned to face the woman who had opened her door without knocking.

"Mrs. Donohugh? We need you out here on the double."

"What's happening? If they're putting me back on camera, I'll need to put on some makeup."

"After last night, I don't think we're on that script anymore. But Mr. Ortega just woke up and we'd like you to help put him at ease."

"If you say so. I don't think seeing *my* face will offer him much comfort though. This DDM has probably been his worst nightmare."

"Hey—are you a part of this team? Have you been watching TV this morning?"

"No. I saw more than enough yesterday, if you

know what I mean."

"The point is, we're *all* in scramble mode here. We just had to arrest ten of Luis's fans when they tried to break in through the garbage facility. So can you just saddle up for us, please?"

"I'll be there in five minutes."

Luis's room was half-filled with hospital staff and business types, but Kate was relieved to see that Ryan Richards was not among them. The group parted as she approached the bed, and a nurse motioned for her to sit beside Luis.

Kate settled into a chair and smiled at him.

"Good morning. It's been quite a week for all of us. How are you feeling?"

"Hi, Kate," Luis said. "I'm okay, just really sleepy."

"Well, you may be the lucky one for having slept through everything else that's happened. Have they told you about yesterday's news?"

"No, they just keep staring at me and whispering. Am I really that sick?"

"Not in the least! And in fact," Kate said, turning toward the others, "do you all need to be in here? How about a little breathing room?"

As most of the people cleared out, one suit leaned in and whispered to Kate, "Keep leading him forward. We've got to find out if he's willing to go to that job site. Do your best to convince him. We *really* need a PR win right now."

The man retreated to a far corner chair and began typing into his phone. One nurse also remained in the room a respectful distance away. Kate turned back toward Luis.

"Now, have they even told you where you are?"

"The nurse said something about South Dakota. Guess I'm still a long way from home."

"Yeah. The Beneficiary-turned-fugitive. Not a good look for the HRA! I don't think the way they caught up to you is playing very well with the public either."

"I was just chilling in the back of the truck. Trying not to get claustrophobic, just thinking about getting home, you know. Then everything got crazy. People running around, sirens, lights—and now I wake up in here."

"So, Luis, that all happened a couple days ago. And yesterday the same hackers who took over our TV show sent another message. As you may remember, I actually work for the HRA, and honestly, we're hurting right now. I think all these people here want a picture of you and me in Cleveland smiling together wearing hard hats."

"Oh, no more, please," Luis groaned. "I'm missing my classes."

"But," Kate said quietly as she leaned in, "I don't really feel like doing that either. So if you keep refusing, I'll try to back you up."

The suit in the corner looked up from his phone and called out, "What are you two whispering about? Is he gonna play ball or not?"

"Sir, I don't think so. Mr. Ortega, who happens to be our Beneficiary guest of honor, insists that completing his studies is a more important priority."

"Is that true, young man?"

Luis adjusted himself higher in the bed. "I need to make my family proud. Some of them already do construction and stuff. I want to do more, get that degree in electrical engineering."

"So you won't go, huh?"

Luis and Kate both stared at the man defiantly. He turned and left the room. The nurse approached and offered Luis a glass of water. He gulped it down and thanked her.

A moment later the suit charged back in followed by an older, more distinguished-looking man. Kate recognized him as an HRA bigwig, whom she might have even briefly met at a function sometime in the past.

The suit dragged a chair to the opposite side of the bed and motioned for the older man to sit. Luis glanced at Kate. She gave a small shrug of her shoulders.

"Well, Luis," the man said, "it's nice to see you're up and no worse for wear."

"Thank you."

"My name's Joshua Gerber. I'm one of the HRA's national directors. Yesterday they flew me out here from DC to see what all the fuss was about. I was in the air when the latest Sentinels of Jubilee nonsense happened. The HRA brass didn't know whether to turn the plane around or what. But you know what I said? 'Let me talk to this brave man, Luis Ortega. Let us have a heart-to-heart and see if we can't come to an understanding.' They agreed, but from what I hear, you insist on not being a part of this great outreach program Construction 4 Community. Is that right?"

"Okay," Luis began, "I'll tell you the same thing I'm saying to all the other people. I'm in college. That's a big deal in my family. I think it's dumb to leave it and waste my time doing manual labor."

"Really now? You don't want poor kids to have a nice new home? Some gratitude…"

"If I may," Kate said. "I think, Mr. Gerber, what Mr. Ortega is trying to say is that his own family comes from an impoverished background. And pursuing this course of higher education is perhaps his own attempt to fulfill the American Dream."

"Is that the deal? And you're his DDM who works for us, right?"

"I know, it sounds like I'm speaking against our own interests. But is the HRA really about us or them? The organization or the Beneficiaries?"

"Of course it's ultimately for them. But there's more to it than one man's fate. There's public perception, for example, and right now we've got another bloody nose! The HRA has already helped his family out financially, so now he's got to do his part to keep the show on the road."

"Isn't there any way that he could continue his studies, but we parlay it so that the HRA still looks good? Show people that we have a heart?

"*Parlay*, did you say? Hmm…"

Gerber rubbed his temples for a moment, then looked up with a satisfied smile.

"Tell me, Luis. How long until you get your degree?"

"It's only an associate's, so like, less than two years."

"Okay, so if we let you defer your DDM assignment, you could fulfill it in 2030."

"You know, Luis," Kate added, "many people pursue a four-year bachelor's degree immediately after getting their associate's. Then there's master's and doctoral programs to consider. In theory, you could be in school for the next ten years!"

Gerber stared daggers at her.

"Thank you, Mrs. Donohugh. I'm sure Mr. Ortega will be able to make up his own mind about such matters."

"I just want him to know all his options. He *is* a Beneficiary, right?"

"Oh, yes. And I've just come up with an idea which might *benefit* all parties involved. Now listen, Luis. I'm happy to let you get back to your studies in California. All I ask is one small favor in return…"

2. WINED AND DINED

"Excuse me, sir?"

Clyde Jenkins felt a tap on his arm. He opened his eyes and saw the flight attendant smiling at him.

"Sorry to wake you," she said, "but we're going to be landing in half an hour. Can I get you anything else before we close up?"

Clyde rubbed his eyes. "Just a little orange juice. Thanks."

He glanced out the window at the patches of clouds scattered above the rocky, desert terrain below. He smiled. Months ago, back in the doldrums of his old life, the view from his mentor Nolan's rooftop in Newark was as far as he could see. But it had given him an inspirational vision, a new thread of hope that he followed until it manifested in the hip-hop song "Fly So High."

This single was a raw and youthful take on the frustrating reality of life for America's poorest, even several years into the nation's formal effort to atone for its colonial past via Reparations. And it had resonated with millions of people, becoming the surprise hit of the summer as it catapulted Clyde's life into the spotlight.

There was no telling where this whirlwind that had saved him from the aimless life of the streets would take him next, but for one moment, as the plane eased downward, Clyde sat back to take in the view. Because right now, he was flying so much higher than he ever imagined was possible for anyone.

After the plane landed and was taxiing toward the gate, the same flight attendant came back into the first-class cabin and leaned down toward him.

"Mr. Jenkins? We've been told that a bit of a crowd has gathered in the terminal. Your escort sent two bodyguards to accompany you as soon as you get off the plane."

"Oh, wow," Clyde said. "They want to see me in the flesh all the way out here?"

"I guess so! Welcome to Los Angeles..."

The scene at LAX may not have been as rabid as when The Beatles passed through, but Clyde was nonetheless impressed to see nearly a hundred people crowded around the terminal exit. Some fans held up signs proclaiming their support or wishing him a happy sweet sixteen. Others proudly shook 3D-printed bobblehead dolls with his likeness.

A handful of people wore bulky metal harnesses equipped with a dozen selfie-stick camera mounts. They had been hired by fans who lived far away or were too socially awkward to leave home, but still wanted the experience of being there in person.

Hovering above the crowd were a few brightly colored QuietDrones which were owned by media outlets. Clyde waved up at them and chuckled. Just as a reporter angled to get a crack at an interview, the two towering bodyguards asserted themselves and briskly led Clyde along the barrier that held back the fans.

He came face to face with a short man in a business suit who was holding a small sign of his own. It read: "Happy (Belated) Birthday, Clyde!"

"There he is!" the man said. "The DJ himself. How was your flight?"

"How you doin', Mr. Pryor? It was a nice trip out."

"Great to hear, great to hear. But please, call me Eddie. We're gonna be good friends."

"Okay, Eddie. Sure thing. Man, this is wild."

Clyde pulled out his phone and started taking pictures of the crowd. One group had begun to chant, "DJC! DJC!" Another group responded with, "Clyde! Clyde! Clyde!"

"Yep," Eddie said, "they really love you. Did Mr. Simmons fly out with you?"

"Nah. Nolan's got a lot going on right now. He wanted to come, but since you and I are just talking…"

"No problem. Come on, let's head to the limo. Did you check a suitcase?"

"Nope. Got all I need in this gym bag."

They loaded up into the car a few minutes later. After the driver shut the doors, Eddie leaned back in his seat and put his hands behind his head. He grinned.

"I'm so glad you made it. First time in LA?"

"Yeah."

"You'll soon find out that the west coast is nothing like how things are back east. Everything is so *constricting* back there! People always on your ass about something. But—if I may paraphrase you—*out here, out here,* people leave you the hell alone if you go with the flow."

"Cool, cool."

The limo left the airport and Clyde watched with

interest as the West Los Angeles streets came into view. Everything was packed together like back home, but the atmosphere still felt more open. There were fewer tall buildings, for one thing. And that bright sun shining on his face through the open window was just electric.

"Is there anything you want to see before you get settled at the hotel?" Eddie asked. "Want to put your toes in the sand? The ocean's only fifteen minutes away!"

"No, thanks. I need to get a shower, take a little rest. Maybe we do that tomorrow before I fly out."

"You're the boss! Here, have a sparkling water."

Clyde closed the window and relaxed, taking occasional glances at the streets as the limo worked its way into Hollywood. Forty-five minutes later they arrived at the Mondrian hotel, where a sharply dressed concierge greeted them and escorted them to the elevator.

"I hope, sir," the concierge said, after opening the doors of an incredibly large penthouse suite, "that you have a wonderful stay with us—up here, up here!"

The concierge walked off with a jump in his step. Clyde shook his head and said, "Being famous is a trip."

"Haha, oh yes," Eddie said. "Everybody puts on a little show for you. That guy wants to be a star too, you know."

Clyde walked to the window and looked out at the Sunset Strip and Hollywood Hills behind it. Fancy houses sat precariously on the edges, often with thin metal poles supporting balconies and garages.

Eddie stood beside him and patted him on the back. "Nice, huh? Some people work in the industry for a long time before they can afford something like that.

People you've never heard of. Animators. Producer's assistants. But I tell ya what—" Eddie rubbed his hands together "—you and I make a nice deal, you'll be in one of those houses next week. And still keep a place back east if you want."

"They look nice, no doubt."

"Throw some parties. Get the girls coming over. Just gotta keep writing hits…"

Clyde turned away back toward the suite.

"But anyway," Eddie said, skipping past him, "plenty of time to dive into that later. Get some rest, young man, and I'll pick you up at six-thirty. We've got reservations right down the street—and *then* we can talk turkey!"

The door clicked shut a moment later and Clyde was alone. He unpacked his bag and brought the toiletries into the bathroom. He brushed his teeth and rinsed his face, then plopped down onto the suite's enormous bed.

"Not bad," he said. "A bed fit for a king."

Clyde closed his eyes and thought about the upcoming evening. First a dinner meeting with Eddie, then a chance to explore the nightlife. See how the LA scene compared to places like Chicago and Atlanta, where the clubs had made him their darling. Little old Clyde, who'd never been on anyone's guest list, was now being comped ornate bottles of liqueur in gated-off VIP sections.

And the girls! No more pleading the neighborhood sisters for attention—they all wanted him now, even the really fine ones. But anytime he felt himself about to lose control and get swept away into the party life, his sister Myra's words of warning echoed in his head. *Don't get no girl pregnant.*

And she would know why. Knocked up at sixteen

with Tyrell by a guy who Clyde barely remembered. Then Octavius got her pregnant two years ago. But at least he came around more often, even threw Clyde some odd jobs before his song blew up this past summer.

But it was really Nolan who helped Clyde keep his wits. He did give Clyde a wide berth at first, when the world suddenly opened up and it was hard to tell who was more starstruck—the fans for Clyde or vice versa.

Nolan accompanied him on trips to the big cities, keeping a cautious eye as Clyde soaked up the glitter of being the man of the hour. Sometimes Clyde ended up doing an impromptu live rendition of his song, and his spirits soared when the audience sang along with the chorus.

But one morning in September, after two days of hard partying in Baltimore, Nolan somehow got into Clyde's suite and put his foot down. First, he told the girl in Clyde's bed to get out. When Clyde protested, Nolan poured him a cup of coffee and told him that play time was over and he should get dressed.

As annoyed as Clyde was to see What's-Her-Name with the curly hair leave, he always trusted Nolan to look out for him, so he didn't say anything and got himself ready. Nolan drove the rental car out of the nice area where they were staying and crossed over into a crumbling part of town that looked just as bad as some of the streets back home in Newark.

All Nolan said during the next hour, as they passed block after blighted block, was "Mm-hmm" and "You see?" Clyde nodded his head, because he did see. The song that had made him famous wasn't about him—it was about the people in broken-down areas across the country who lived his message: that Reparations was not achieving what it set out to do.

At one point, Nolan stopped the car at a dingy intersection and they looked around. An old woman shuffled down the sidewalk while pushing a mesh cart with a misshapen wheel. Trash and dead branches clogged a gutter grate. Guys in layers of sweats smoked cigarettes and moved from one boarded-up storefront to another. And a small makeshift memorial of glass candle, flowers, and a picture frame lay tipped over next to a stop sign.

When an HRA mini-drone came into view and hovered over the intersection like a hummingbird, Nolan tilted his head toward Clyde and raised his eyebrows. Clyde nodded. Nolan put the car in drive and took him back to the hotel.

After that Baltimore trip, Clyde found that Nolan was less and less available to act as chaperon when he traveled. But he had gotten the message, and made a point of meeting up with locals in small groups, talking to them, listening to their stories. He absorbed their praise of his song humbly and with gratitude, and found that in the evenings he didn't want to party so much anymore.

Because he had work to do. A responsibility to these people. And a new song to write.

But even after refocusing, Clyde still struggled to find a message as important as the one in "Fly So High." It wasn't even that he was afraid of being a one-hit wonder—that was a common fate in this era of instant downloads and short attention spans. But the world was actually listening to what an everyday Beneficiary had to say right now, and DJ Clydoscope did not want to squander that opportunity. Nolan often reminded him of this, and the responsibility weighed on him.

After waking up from his nap, Clyde showered and put on his maroon suit. He looked at himself in the mirror and was impressed—but couldn't help wondering if he really deserved all that Eddie Pryor was offering. This top-tier agent had a roster of professional artists that made Clyde feel way out of his league. But Eddie had been very persistent over the past month, so Nolan agreed that Clyde should at least listen to his pitch.

"Worst case," Nolan had said, "it'll open your eyes a bit more. Best case, you get to take your message big time for real."

The limo arrived promptly at six-thirty and drove them west down Sunset. The early fall twilight gave Clyde a taste of what Saturday nights on this famous strip must look like, but for now it was mostly the dinner crowd that was out.

They pulled up to a row of restaurants about a mile away from the hotel. There was fancy Italian, a sushi joint, and a brewpub with a wood-fired oven. Eddie led Clyde down the sidewalk to a place whose logo featured two capital *R*'s sitting back to back. The front of the building was brick accented by shiny brass.

As they entered, Clyde could see through the dim lighting several dozen glowing teal tubes made of frosted glass. They were spaced evenly throughout the entire establishment, from the lobby to the dining area and back into the kitchen.

A skinny man, whose jet-black hair had a green streak down the middle, glided toward them. He adjusted the keychain zipper at the top of his faux-leather shirt and beamed.

"Welcome to RestauRoom! Do you have a reservation?"

"Yes, we do," Eddie said. "Under Pryor."

"Oh, but of course! We have a private booth over in the corner, just as you requested. Follow me, please."

As they entered the seating area, Clyde saw one of the tall neon tubes swivel open. A man stepped out, and the glass closed again as he walked away.

And when Clyde's party reached their booth, the tube right next to their table also opened, and again someone came out. Clyde watched as this woman made her way to the other side of the dining room, where she sat down at a table and joined the conversation.

He turned to the host. "What's up with all these sliding doors?"

"First time here, sir?"

Eddie patted Clyde on the back. "Visiting from back east."

"Oh, my! Welcome, then! You are in for a real treat. RestauRoom is the world's first and only all-accommodating, gender-inclusive dining establishment. We have facilities for thirty-four different pronouns, plus three rotating tubes over by the bar for wandering genders."

Clyde pointed to the monolith of curved glass beside him. "So this is a toilet right here? Next to where I'm supposed to eat?"

"It was the only way. This ain't wide-open Texas, cowboy. Between high real estate prices and limited space here on Sunset, we had to utilize absolutely every square inch. Retrofitting was simply out of the question, so we hired the legendary Toronto designer Elephon to bring our vision to life. Xe did a fabulous job intertwining the layout, don't you think? Efficient and elegant!"

"It doesn't smell bad, at least," Clyde mumbled.

"Don't be silly! Each chute is equipped with an

eight-stage air filter and Bose noise-canceling technology. Belize me, what happens in tube, stays in tube!"

"So how do I know which one to use?"

"You see those girls walking around carrying shooter trays? Find one of them, order a shot—if you want, that is—and they'll help you locate the cubbyhole which best serves your current gender."

"I think he gets it," Eddie said. "Let's have a seat. Thank you."

Clyde settled into the round booth and surveyed the restaurant. He saw a man exit the tube beside the reception station and immediately shake someone's hand. He looked over at Eddie.

"You like this place?"

"Oh yeah! My clients come from *all* walks of life. And RestauRoom has the facilities to meet their needs. As I like to say," Eddie added, tapping the glass tube beside him with a large gold ring, "the teal seals the deal!"

A moment later, this door rotated open and a woman with shaved head and giant purple ear gauges poked her head out.

"Sorry, sorry," Eddie said. The door closed again.

"How's the food here?" Clyde asked.

"It's excellent. The best!"

"What do they mean when they say this?" Clyde looked down and read from the menu, "Diversify your digestion with our ethno-fluid entrees."

"That just means they have it all, pal. You want free-range chicken, they got it. Fair-trade tofu, no problem. *And* they use separate preparation areas in case you're allergic—divided by a wall of peanuts, of course, hahaha! Just kidding, oh boy..."

"I'll probably just have a burger."

"Ahhh, here we go, right on time!"

A server had arrived with a bottle of champagne. After she poured their drinks and withdrew, Eddie raised his glass and smiled.

"A toast to the rising star. DJ Clydoscope, may all of your wishes come true!"

"Cheers, Eddie. I appreciate all the effort you're making to show me a good time."

A few minutes later, after they'd ordered their dinners, Eddie brought his fingertips together.

"Okay, young man, here's the deal. Your song, it was brilliant. As if in that golden moment of inspiration, you were touched by the hand of God. But —can you do it again?"

"I hope so," Clyde said. "I plan to."

"How long has it been now? Three, four months? What else have you written? Most guys who make it have at least a few other decent tracks ready to go."

Clyde looked down. He said, "The old ones aren't so good. I'm trying to get the lyrics right for the next song."

"Clyde, we're losing time here. With every week that passes, your window to seize on this momentum shrinks. By January people will be like, 'Clyde who?' You've got so much potential to springboard to the next level right now. We can't let it go to waste."

"I mean, I'm close. Kind of. Maybe another month, I'll be ready."

Eddie stabbed at his ice water with a straw.

"How would you feel," he said, "if I told you I've already got it all set up? Five tracks completely written. A studio at my disposal, day or night. And videographers on call. We could do this thing tomorrow!"

"Five songs? About what?"

"Oh, you know. The HRA being crap. The president being a failure. How much you love your family and hate to see them suffer."

"My family?" Clyde drew back in his seat.

"Yeah! Heartstrings stuff. But not just that. My stylists can mock up a whole new look for you—wardrobe, hats, jewelry, everything. Hey, do you like Bekki Triage?"

Clyde nodded. "She aight."

"Great!" Pryor said. "We could have you two walk down Rodeo Drive together. Maybe you even give her a peck on the cheek—it's okay, she'll be in on it—and our photographer will send some pics over to *TMZ*. *Then* DJ Clydoscope will get that promotional boost that only Eddie P. can deliver!"

Eddie grabbed his champagne and sat back against the booth, smirking as he gave a firm nod.

"Hold on," Clyde said. "I respect that you know how to make singers get big. It's a honor being here with you. But what does me flirtin' with Bekki have to do with my music?"

"Clyde," Eddie said, "you've been the male version of Cinderella for a little while now. The poor boy from New Jersey—the upstart, the mystery man. And Bekki is hip-hop *royalty!* This rumor of a fling will cement you as a force to be reckoned with. And right then, we hit 'em with your next track! In fact, we've got a timely little ditty that I even helped to write. It's called 'Non Compos Presidentis.' Eh?"

Clyde wiped his mouth with a napkin, then exhaled.

"I get it," he said. "You're trying to take things to the next level. But this is my actual life, Eddie. I'm just Clyde, you know? I found the people—or they found me—because what I did was real. It was genuine, from the heart. But acting like I have a famous girlfriend or singing another angry song just because? I don't know…"

Eddie shook his head quickly from side to side, then said, "How can I make you see what's there for the taking? You're gonna be at thirteen million downloads by the election. Drop the new track dissing Jeffries-Lao next week, and you'll sell a million copies out the gate! It's time to cash in on the people's rage. Come on."

"But it's so much bigger than me." Clyde gritted his teeth. "My people need more than rage. Things got to move forward. 'Cause you know, the government already gave us money, so what's more of that gonna do?"

"Clyde, Clyde. That's all well and good. I love your idealism, believe me. But we've got to think about your image. The DJC brand was built on a special kind of anger that's not blind, but righteous! Don't go soft on me and we can make this work."

" 'Go soft,' that's funny. Everything's about image, isn't it? The *impression* of who you are and how people react. Playing a part. Like the pissed-off Beneficiary, right?"

"That's what got you here." Eddie shrugged his shoulders. "And it's my job to read people's minds. I've been in the business long enough to have my finger on that pulse."

"Then why didn't you just cook up someone like me in the lab six months ago? If you already know what's up?" Clyde raised his eyebrows.

Eddie squeezed his hand into a fist and shook it. "Clyde. You erupted like a volcano out of the ocean and created a whole new island. It was a beautiful thing. But now my job is to populate the place and bring in the tourists. So unless you've already prepared a ten-year business plan that maps out your character arc…"

"Ten years? I can't think that far ahead. I don't even know what kind of inspiration I'll find at the beach tomorrow."

"My man. Here's some real talk. Every day, five million would-be artists also have their moment of inspiration. They snap a nice picture or record a homemade track, and then they throw it out into the ether. Guess what? It just floats away and fades into nothingness. To be a star with lasting power today, you need more than a dream or even a plan. You need a fully scripted identity!"

"I *do not* follow you," Clyde said. "I mean, you want to hire some ghostwriters to try to recreate my vibe? Yeah, I kinda get that. But what's up with trying to change me into something else?"

"Okay, buddy," Eddie said with a sigh. "We're getting in deep now. Maybe I shouldn't tell you all this if it's gonna burst your bubble, but if you want in on the biz—"

"Well, that I don't know. I mean, I've been havin' a good time since the summer. But like you said, I'm a new island."

"Let's pick it apart, see if you can absorb this. Here's how my world operates. You know how royal families arrange marriages to create alliances and keep up appearances?"

"I guess, maybe," Clyde said.

"Well, here in entertainment we do a similar kind of thing. Why? Because we're not just selling movie tickets! It's also celebrity lifestyles, the drama of their relationships and breakups, even their scandals. The sad fall from grace followed by the touching moment of redemption—all caught on camera for the world to see. We're talking clicks, page views, magazine readership, TV specials. We're getting people hooked on a star's brand as loyal customers for however many decades they're in the business."

"Wow…"

Eddie waved his arm across the table slowly.

"Celebrity cosmetics, clothing lines, end-of-life memoirs, all of it. You see, the side hustles pay for the big show! But the best part of it is this. Remember that concierge at the hotel earlier today? He and all the restaurant staff right here, they're banging their heads against the wall trying to figure out how to break in. And you! You just appeared like the Virgin Mary bestowing miracles on the masses. And yet from what I hear tonight, you're thinking about walking away on a technicality? Because your art has a message? That's crazy talk!"

"Well, maybe you don't know who I am then," Clyde said. " 'Cause if I'm miraculous like you say, maybe I have a bigger mission in life than being some pretty boy."

Eddie threw his hands up. "Clyde, I flew you out here because I like you. And my team wants to work with you. If I dropped too much knowledge tonight, I apologize. I don't want to scare you away. But I do want you to take the next step, whatever it may be, with eyes open. I can't be responsible if you have a mental breakdown three years from now because this whole deal wasn't what you expected it to be. Heh, you aren't supposed to freak out until *after* you turn twenty-one anyway…"

Clyde took the napkin from his lap and folded it neatly. "Mr. Pryor, thank you very much for the dinner. I think I'll go back to my hotel now."

"Oh, come on!" Eddie pleaded. "No hard feelings. But this is the Sunset Strip! Don't crash out on me, please. We've got a VIP table set up over at Club

Fortuna."

"Man, I don't know. This is all getting to be too much."

"Clyde. Give 'em one hour. Some of your fans paid a pretty penny for that access. Have a little taste of what fame from coast to coast is like. No more talk about business, I promise. I just want to make sure there aren't any blind spots when you fly home."

"Alright. I'll check it out."

"That's the spirit, kid! Do you need to take a leak before we go?"

Clyde looked around the dining room from tube to tube, then smiled. "Nah… I'll just hold it til we get to the club."

"Saturday night! Hollywood! DJC in the house!"

Eddie drained his cocktail and flagged down the server.

3. THE SENTINELS

The group sat in near darkness. Two dim lamps created silhouettes of the eight men seated around the room.

The man sitting at a desk near the shaded window broke the silence. "Nine days since we announced ourselves to the world. And none of our operatives have blown their cover."

"Here, here," a voice from across the room called out.

"Now, it's three weeks until the election. New polling indicates a tightening race which the president will still likely win, so tonight we will discuss our action plan leading up to Election Day. We've already established back-channel contact with both campaigns, but beyond that it's up to the voters. Now, gentlemen, what's the first order of business?"

Another man rose from his seat and approached the window. An outside light cast soft yellow across the edge of his face.

"Congressman," he said, "first let me offer my utmost respect for everything you've put on the line to be a part of this movement. The word 'courageous' might be used too often when a politician crosses party lines, but in your case it rings very true."

"I appreciate your kind words," the man at the desk said. "Please continue."

"When we found each other one year ago, coming together from all walks of life, our common bond was concern for the direction our country was headed. From our respective high perches, we saw lethargy and demoralization creeping across people's faces.

"Whichever way you look at it, this was a bad trend. Bad for business. Bad for our children. Bad for morale in the military. Reparations, which sought to rectify one thing, was in fact creating an enormous new tear across the fabric of this nation.

"And so we joined forces—not as a cabal or to pull off a coup—but in an attempt to take the more noble aspects of the Reparations sentiment to a more mature level. We have scored two major victories on the world stage this month, so perhaps now is a good time to assess where we are."

"If I may?" a new voice said from one of the armchairs.

"Please do, Admiral."

"My assets have been able to assemble over twenty thousand military veterans from around the country to help keep an eye on the situation. I'll admit, reports are that some of these guys are in pretty bad shape. Many were recruited from homeless encampments, in fact. But overall, they seem ready and willing to help keep the peace should things get out of hand on Main Street."

"Thank you," the man at the window said. "Who's next?"

A man seated at a small table rapped his knuckles

against the surface. "Sales are down," he grumbled. "And they've been down across all industries. Who the hell wants to buy a sports car when people will look at you with suspicion for enjoying it? White or black, it doesn't matter."

"Here, here!"

"I don't care who wins the election. We need to work with whoever's president to get business moving again. Retail sales for the Holy Holidays are going to be atrocious this year. And yes, I know other factors contributed to this slump. Automation, AI, and people just holed up playing with their gadgets. But I swear, the HRA has thrown cold water into everyone's face, and people are not spending a dime because they're so tied up in knots. We gotta fix this."

"Absolutely," the congresshuman said. "Rest assured that I have been quietly discussing the economy with several of my trusted colleagues on both sides of the aisle. And when the dust settles on this election, I plan to make a passionate speech on the House floor echoing these sentiments—if not explicitly, then in words that a Dramacrat would be expected to use."

"That's all I ask. For more of the same teamwork that's gotten us so far and shocked the world already."

A man in the far corner of the room cleared his throat. "I would like to say a few words."

The man at the window stepped back into the darkness and said, "You have the floor, Your Prescience."

"Thank you. While I may not have been among your ranks this whole time, I feel that I've gotten to know you quite well over the past several months. I'm honored that you would tap me to be the... face, as it were, when announcing the existence of the Sentinels of Jubilee."

"And our judgment was validated by how well you've carried yourself. Particularly during the live broadcasts. Your mask added to the mystery, even if you wear it for your own reasons. We're all holding our breath in anticipation of your next speech."

"In truth, that is why I asked to be heard tonight. I believe that most of what needs to be done to push back against the HRA now rests with the people. They must take back control of these tools which were supposed to make our lives easier, but which have instead enslaved us to the multi-tasking treadmill.

"But until that existential declaration begins, I don't see how anything else I might say would be of use. Therefore I regrettably must use this occasion to announce my retirement from active duty, and to return to my own obligations as religious leader."

"Just like that, huh?" a man who so far had not spoken groaned. "What are we gonna do for a spokesman if he leaves?"

"Remember," the admiral said, "we have all respected the fact that anyone who serves can only give what they are able to."

"I know, I know. But I don't understand how *he* in particular can bring himself to walk away at just this moment. Your Prescience, MARVIN is your brainchild —is it not?—and the government stole it from you. But by working with us, you've been able to take back the reins!"

"First," the Prescient One said, "I still have my own organization to run—"

"As do we all."

"And while I will neither confirm nor deny whether that operating system is my creation, the bigger point is this: the cat is already out of the bag on the idea that massive databases can enable punitive worldviews to grow to terrible proportions. It goes far beyond MARVIN now. We're too late to stop it by years! I truly hope you gentlemen are able to put your diverse experience in business and politics to good use as you try to steer the transition. But my most relevant abilities would go to waste as a technical director."

"But what are you going to do?" the man pleaded, rising from his chair. "Just wander off and live out your days in that old shopping mall?"

"I assure you that it would be impossible to return to my former life unaffected. This unique group has taught me to take my position more seriously. I promise to do my part to meet you in the middle someday soon. We all have profound work to do. Mod bless you."

"Come on, Prescient! Don't get mystical with us right at the end. We love you, buddy, and I know that Scott is in there somewhere buried under that getup of yours."

"Now, now," someone called out. "How much has he had to drink? Jesus…"

"I'm just saying, we've worked side by side but still he won't trust us enough to show his face without some sort of damn prosthetic spackled on. We're *all* complicit here. It's just, he's done an incredible job and I hate to see him go."

"This use of familiarity," the Prescient One said, "I will accept as camaraderie after serving on this secret mission together. But the Sentinels' major offensive is over, and in victory you can now map out the occupation. I have my own priorities to attend to, so forgive me if I cannot yet join you in such casual talk. Until that day, thank you one and all."

A short while later, after the meeting had adjourned

and the men waited for their drivers to pull up the gravel road, the admiral felt a tap on his shoulder.

"Excuse me," the man in a long cloak and wearing an eggshell blue mask said, "I recall you saying that a number of the military veteran Sentinels are not well?"

"That's correct. Broken down bodies neglected by Veterans Affairs. Spirits thrown under the bus and crushed by the family courts. A lot of substance abuse and despair during cold nights with nowhere to stay. Thank God we've gotten them out of the shanty towns, but I doubt they'll be of any use to us tactically."

"If I may, I would like to extend an offer of a comfortable place for some of them to recuperate."

"That's very generous. But... this isn't some Modestian recruiting tactic, is it? I don't think it would do them any good to live inside that mall of yours."

"You have my word that this invitation is strictly humanitarian. Consider it a parting gift to the Sentinels. I own several properties which have been converted into convalescent homes. It would be an honor for these warriors to find some comfort after all this time out in the wilderness."

"I do appreciate your gesture. Let me make some inquiries and I'll be in touch. Ah, it looks like that's me here. Take care of yourself."

The two men shook hands and the admiral got into the back seat of a limousine. The man in the cloak watched the car drive off, then looked up at the starry night sky that was so vibrant above this isolated country estate.

After arriving at the commuter airport and embarking on his jet, the Prescient One removed his costume. Moving into the bathroom, he next took out the patterned contact lenses he habitually wore to defeat biometric cameras.

He looked at his unvarnished face in the mirror. Just another man of forty. A few wrinkles. Some stubble. More bags under the eyes than one would want to see. But the Prescient One had great responsibilities, and was under added strain trying to juggle his role as religious leader with his more recent membership among the Sentinels.

During his absence from the Mall of Absolution, which had been explained to the congregation as a spiritual sabbatical, he gave weekly sermons by video. Meanwhile, the church's high-ranking members oversaw life at the Mall.

Even prior to the first Sentinels hack, these leaders had told him that the church's ranks were starting to swell—but after that fateful initial broadcast on *DDM TV Live*, hundreds of people spooked out of their wits by the masked man's message began to arrive seeking asylum. The church was simply not equipped to handle such an influx of refugees without its leader on hand.

And though the Prescient One had not wanted to leave his post with the Sentinels until after the election, the fact that his own speeches on their behalf had put this pressure on his church, strongly influenced his decision to return home now.

As he settled into the divan on his private jet, the Prescient One wondered how long it had been since someone last addressed him by his formal name. Scott Cullen. Who the world first came to know in 2010 when he released *Thor's Tablet*, a revolutionary video game which merged all the hallmarks of fantasy lore into a modern setting, complete with real-time data gathered from cameras around the world.

This massively popular game vaulted him out of dorm-room isolation and into the arms of nerdy Comic-

Con girls, as well as online fashion models whose nose for money and fame overlooked his awkward mannerisms. Several years of running with that beach-and-booze crowd served to smooth out these personality quirks.

But then, wealthy beyond his ability to spend and all partied out, Scott changed focus in time to be a prime mover in the blockchain revolution. Whereas the general population got caught up in the cryptocurrency craze looking to make a quick buck, he was obsessed with the technology's underlying premise: decentralized, permissionless information that was impervious to the kind of corruption that had enabled the Pentagon to lose track of trillions of dollars without being held accountable.

His wisdom and experience served as a beacon for people creating their own blockchain-related businesses and products, when public awareness about the technology reached a tipping point in 2019-20. Meanwhile, the prime targets of blockchain's amoral wrath—government, military, and financial institutions —could only resist for so long. And when the American Mortgage Brokers Association later announced its intention to go "full blockchain," Scott officially declared victory and embarked on another yearlong partying binge.

Sometime during the winter of 2022-23, after he had returned from a Scandinavian backpacking expedition, he received a meeting request from a delegation of Dramacrat politicians and grassroots activists called the Colonial Amends Committee. Always up for new ideas and opportunities, Scott readily accepted. Not only did this meeting help refocus his mind on work, but one of the group's professional members sold him on their pitch.

"You've gone from cashing in on heroes and princesses," the man had said, "to battling the real-life dragon of systemic corruption. And yes, even though a lot of everyday people got rich following your lead with the cryptos, the truth is that many others are still hurting out there. Are you ready to work on something revolutionary that will help them?"

And so Scott Cullen began working on what would later become the main tool of the Historical Reparations Administration. He was hired as project leader with full supervisory powers, but soon found that operating within the government's hierarchy entailed much different nuances compared to life in the private sector. Gaming and cryptos had always been fueled by an almost standoffish, but still good-natured sense of one-upmanship—and that competitive atmosphere led to major breakthroughs that came at light speed, but often at the expense of feelings.

Scott sensed while working on Project MARVIN that programs stemming from a socially conscious viewpoint appeared to be less goal-oriented, with ample time being devoted to situational pulse-taking to ensure that everyone felt equally appreciated along the journey.

This agonizingly slow and inefficient process of patting everyone on the head resulted in numerous coding errors that later had to be fixed by the most competent techs. Delays and missed deadlines were a matter of course.

Everything came to a head for Scott in the summer of 2025. He and his development team were reviewing the latest system capabilities for several administrative types who dropped in every so often, when a seemingly innocent question about the program's termination date came up.

One of these bureaucrats paused momentarily before saying that she didn't foresee it ever ending. "If we have such a complete database, what would be the point of ever shutting it down? MARVIN will know everything, right? He can be the Alexandria Library on one hand, but also with the power to comprehensively judge. Besides, it's not like bad people have stopped committing crimes, right?"

Scott was so stunned by this unwitting admission that he could barely ask a follow-up question, let alone articulate the terrifying implications of what they were about to unleash. In the sleepless nights that followed, he began to understand how this idealistic accounting project would inevitably become a monolithic tool of vengeance, which lashed out blindly without context or other sympathetic considerations.

He foresaw that even as restitution milestones were reached over time, the system itself would never feel the human satisfaction that justice had been served. The insatiable bots would crawl on and on, perhaps going so far as to deduce more crimes within the scope of reasonable doubt when they ran out of clear-cut evidence to prosecute.

Scott went through the formal channels to voice his fears. But with the government so close to fulfilling this main campaign promise of the nation's first female president, not only were his cries of warning ignored, he was in fact forcefully removed from the project. Then a coordinated series of hit pieces against him appeared in the media. He was called "insane," accused of being a "closet racist," and the final verdict was that "this former tech wunderkind probably fears his own family's sordid past being uncovered."

Had he been younger, or had the project been closer to his heart, he might have fought back to defend his reputation. But that eagle's view which the highly successful tend to attain told him it was better to recede while he pondered all of the ramifications—rather than to simply send off a series of whiny posts on social media.

With an open heart, Scott retreated to his cabin in Colorado and contemplated the meaning of his life within the context of the macro events playing out. These meditations proved to be the seed of what blossomed into a new religion called Modestianity. He then christened himself as "the Prescient One" and dedicated his church to serve as a shield for people alienated by modern life.

This message proved timely, and the Prescient One began to grow such a large following from all walks of life, that he drew down on his fortune and paid cash for the entire former Mall of America complex. Abandoned in 2022 due to economic conditions that had wreaked havoc across the entire retail sector, the Mall had been both playground and war zone for Somali gangs until its sale to the church in 2026.

These Modestians moved into the enormous facility and went about removing graffiti, bleaching out blood stains, and laying the groundwork for the breathtaking American Mecca that it soon became. Two years later and Modestianity was a fast-growing religion that boasted nearly two hundred smaller chapels around the country.

This all gave Scott Cullen solace at the end of a roller coaster ride which had forced him to endure disgrace, cost him his identity, and nearly pushed his country to the brink of anarchy.

The plane landed at the small airport near St. Paul where the Prescient One owned a hangar. With his face fully cloaked, he quickly transferred into the church helicopter that was waiting, and was soon airborne once again. A short while later, when the Mall of Absolution came into view, he rubbed his hands together with glee.

The chopper touched down on the rooftop helipad. As the door swung open and the Prescient One stepped out wearing fresh makeup, several emissaries and proponents ran up to greet him.

"Ah, Your Prescience," they fawned. "We have missed you so!"

"And I as well. Tell me," he said to an emissary as they passed through sliding doors, "how have you all comported yourselves?"

"Most honorably, sir," the man said. "You will be so very proud of how we have maintained order in your absence."

"So, no power struggles to fill the void?"

"Heavens, no! That you would even consider the —"

"Now, now," the Prescient One said, giving the man a pat on the back. "Just a little gallows humor after so much time on the outside."

They took an elevator down to the lowest level. The doors opened onto his private sanctuary, a room where thousands of blue pieces of fabric dangled from the ceiling.

"You see," a proponent said, casting his arm out, "we've left everything as it was."

"Ah, my lovely vines! How wonderful."

The Prescient One rushed into the thicket and disappeared. The proponent chased after him, saying, "Not to spoil your private homecoming, but word has gotten out regarding your return. The people are eager to see you. Perhaps you could make an appearance this evening?"

The Prescient One poked his head out of the fabric. "Boo!" he shouted with a laugh. "My, my. Please do forgive my folly. But it feels so good to be back in my nest. As to your question, I had already planned to give several formal addresses this week. But yes, I am happy to make a brief speech later."

That evening the main amphitheater was thronged with thousands of chanting members from all stations within the church—access had been granted randomly by instant electronic lottery. For those not lucky enough to attend in person, the event was broadcast on the many large video screens located throughout the Mall.

Several prominent members made introductory remarks, then trumpets heralded the Prescient One's return. He wore a magnificent blue cape whose fifteen-foot train was carried by half a dozen female novitiates. His face was painted silver. Tiny blue fish descended from each eye.

The cheering of the crowd was overwhelming. For people who had joined the church recently, this was their first time seeing the Prescient One in person. There was, however, no way of knowing who among the many crying tears of joy were new members or old.

"Greetings from an old friend," he began. "I know that the messages I sent during my sabbatical did not have the electricity of the real experience, but it is clear to me that all is well here at home. It is a testament to you and the church leadership. I salute you all!"

The audience responded warmly as he turned and bowed to the hundred church officials also on stage.

"Perhaps you sense a more serious tone from me tonight. I have returned from my journey a better man. Reaffirmed and more focused than ever. But I cannot take the next steps alone. I say to those of you who once came here seeking respite from the madness of this world, are you ready to apply the teachings you have absorbed?

"Because now a fresh wave of techno-refugees has arrived, and they are in worse shape than you ever were. Prove yourselves worthy of the shelter we once provided to you, by extending a hand to those now desperately in need of solace. Go out into the corridors lined with cots, or the fields of tents and RVs, and offer them food and a kind word.

"Whether you have taken formal vows or not, the Church of Modestianity has faith in you to assist your human brothers and sisters. Because this is not simply about recruiting members to our ranks—Modestianity exists today because there was a pressing need for a philosophy that looked at the present in order to face the future, rather than looking backward for guidance today.

"And while you rise to the challenge of this task, in the coming weeks and months our church shall also embark on a critical new mission. Because my recent sabbatical bore the fruit of an elegant vision of how to shine our hopeful rays across this nation which is in such pain.

"But that is all yet to come. Forgive me if I must retire so soon, but my odyssey was long and arduous. Be patient, attend to your duties, and I promise that in time your faithfulness shall be rewarded.

"The Church of Modestianity is strong, from the emissaries on down to the lay members, because of you. Whenever you honor yourself through circumspect behavior, you send a healing breath into the world. Each robust discussion about how to protect human dignity within the technological maelstrom, helps to forge the body of wisdom that is the foundation on which our religion will rise ever higher.

"It stirs my soul to not be forgotten by my acolytes. Your faith in me renews my commitment to honor you through good deeds and forthrightness. I will always strive to use my gift of prescience as a guiding light, so that we may thrive in the sweet spot between pride and humility.

"It brings me joy to finally say this in person once again. Mod bless you!"

4. GLOVES OFF

Selected excerpts from the presidential debate held at Indiana University on October 18, 2028.

Moderator: Good evening. I'm Tad Hauer, host of MBC's *News Burst*. Tonight we conduct the third and final presidential debate between Dramacrat incumbent Eileen Jeffries-Lao and Rebellican challenger Victor Dominguez. First, we will hear a brief opening statement from each candidate. Madam President, we start with you.

Jeffries-Lao: Thank you, Tad. It has been my greatest honor to serve as President of the United States. While there was much fanfare made about my gender and race during the previous election, I sincerely believe that our most significant achievements have taken place in the years since that historic victory.

The establishment of the HRA was truly a landmark moment in American history. It signified a turning point in the maturation of our nation's soul, when we finally found the courage to face our deepest historical wounds. And looking forward, perhaps the HRA can serve as a shining city on a hill—if I may paraphrase Ronald Reagan—as the concept of Reparations inspires other nations that also have imperfect track records on race.

We've already done so much, but in many ways we've only just begun. So despite the recent setbacks, you can rest assured that my administration will continue to lead the charge. Re-elect me on November seventh and let's finish the job.

Hauer: Thank you. Mr. Dominguez?

Dominguez: Ladies and gentlemen, for those of you who have followed my campaign or watched the previous debates, you might be surprised to hear me going a bit off script tonight. Sadly, the truth may be that the Rebellican Party nominated me in the spirit of past challengers like Bob Dole, Walter Mondale, and John Kerry. Candidates who were thrown into the ring to put on a decent show, but who in no way were actually going to win. And today, that same network of Washington insiders doesn't want me evicting this incumbent and her team. Why? Because the president hasn't been in town long enough to reward all of her donors with favors!

But after the truly disturbing events we've seen these past eleven days regarding the security of the HRA, one thing has become clear to me and my trusted advisers. Beneath the Dramacrats' eternal good intentions, there has been a dangerous failure of leadership which cannot be allowed another risky four years in power. Whether you agree or disagree with the HRA, it is a massive program that has already sprouted many roots—and it is clear that the president is not capable of running it securely, transparently, and—dare I say—equitably.

Our nation suddenly finds itself on the brink of disaster due to the latest in the Left's seemingly endless series of Utopian experiments. This too threatens, in the end, to make everything worse. Thus I, Victor Dominguez, lowly first-term senator from Arizona, who many people wrote off as the Rebellicans desperately pandering for Latiz-American votes... I hereby declare my sincere intention to go for the knockout punch on Election Day!

Hauer: Our first question tonight does indeed touch on the HRA's recent troubles. Mr. Dominguez, if elected, what would be your plan to right the ship?

Dominguez: Let me first state this for the record. While most of my Rebellican colleagues did not vote in support of the HRA three-and-a-half years ago, I have no intention of disbanding the program. If I'm elected president, the first thing I would do is shore up security, both on the human and digital fronts. It's a disgrace that this centralized database of all Americans' information could be vulnerable to any hack, let alone the terrifying spectacle we've just seen. Like my plumber father, I will get down and dirty if that's what it takes to clear out this mess!

Beyond that, the negative sentiment that was festering among some Caucmericans, and which has now boiled over into this renegade group called the Sentinels of Jubilee... We must seriously consider whether the HRA is functioning as advertised, as well as do more testing and analysis before we decide how to manage the program moving forward.

Rest assured that as president, I will not take any rash steps without consulting both parties, policy analysts, and of course, the American people.

Hauer: President Jeffries-Lao, your response?

Jeffries-Lao: Yes, thank you. After months and months of just going through the motions, tonight we finally see the real Candidate Dominguez that was hiding behind the facade. Less than three weeks before the election and he springs the ultimate flip flop. Tell me, sir, who are you? No, better yet, tell the American people! Because how can you say that you won't make any rash decisions, when you've just pulled this Jekyll and Hyde on us here tonight? Frankly, I'm nervous what you might do with your finger on MARVIN's power switch.

Now, let me be clear. I take the recent troubles at the HRA very seriously. Right now, as they have been doing for the last eleven days, our technicians are working with the FBI and DHS to seal every leak, isolate every rogue actor, and bring the criminal Sentinels of Jubilee to swift justice.

Frankly, I can't believe the petty and shortsighted attitude of all these HRA critics who have popped up in droves, seemingly overnight. Only four years ago, our nation was united in the glow of defying the odds to create perhaps the most tectonic civilizational shift towards good in one hundred seventy-five years. Have we forgotten that everything in life requires fortitude to get through the gritty day-to-day process? Did Eisenhower shut down construction of the national highway network because one tractor got a flat tire? Did FDR abandon the Hoover Dam project because a worker broke his leg?

My goodness, folks. Skeptics may think that I'm so passionate because my name and legacy are forever tied to the HRA, but in my heart I'm thinking about the millions of Beneficiaries we've helped here at home, as well as future Beneficiaries around the world waiting anxiously for their governments to follow our lead. In three weeks, do the sensible thing and re-elect me to finish the job.

Dominguez: It's funny. We have a Chinese-

American president overseeing and cheerleading for a program that does very little for people of her own ancestry.

Hauer: Now, now—

Jeffries-Lao: There he is, Jekyll and Hyde. I wonder how big *his* Reparations checks are...

Hauer: Please! I insist that we move on to the next question. Senator Dominguez, despite what the headlines might suggest, there's more going on in America than all things Reparations. The economy continues to sputter forward, with seemingly every new breakthrough followed by a pullback. So far, you've campaigned on a policy of embracing innovation while ensuring a safety net for the less affluent and less skilled. Does the as-of-tonight Candidate Dominguez have any new thoughts on the matter?

Dominguez: Haha, well... Yes and no.

Hauer: Do tell.

Dominguez: During my two terms as mayor of Flagstaff, I was committed to welcoming small businesses that were tired of being seen as a blood donor by fiscally irresponsible states bogged down in the swamp of debt-ridden pension plans. This policy was a net boon to our city and state. Plus, it put those Dramacrat strongholds on notice that there was an alternative to their overpromise-and-tax mentality.

In addition to my pro-business approach, I have always been aware of the delicate balance between innovation, acclimation, and obsolescence that characterizes the flow of progress in a capitalistic society. Prior to this century, workers could often expect their field of expertise to be relevant throughout their working lives. But the exponential disruption we've witnessed since 2000 makes it almost impossible for everyday people to achieve the stability necessary to live out the American Dream: homeownership, stable communities, and meaningful work.

Still, we cannot risk stunting the creative spirit that bursts forth across the country. Sacrificing the innovative spark for comfort is not the answer. So if the president wants a taste of the new me, I believe that concepts like Reparations, when taken too far, reveal an alarming truth about the Left. As if their core philosophy could be defined as an obsession with dividing up the contents of the pantry equally among all people, but at the same time completely ignoring the need to produce, adapt, and grow in preparation for the future.

Hauer: Thirty seconds…

Dominguez: Yes. The Dramacrats have long championed welfare and universal basic income as ways to protect the most economically vulnerable among us. I would also like to propose grants or setting up campuses for people born with the fire to create, so that their contributive abilities and visionary skills are not stunted by the drudgery of rote education, or even monthly bills if necessary. The nation—if not humankind itself—will surely benefit from unleashing these great minds.

Hauer: Interesting proposal. Sort of a genius career track, or something like a sports league's development system, for lack of a better metaphor. Mrs. Jeffries-Lao?

Jeffries-Lao: He's thrown so much out there, where do I begin? I assume his mention of underfunded pensions was a veiled jab at my home state of California—as if we haven't all borne the brunt of that across the nation. Nearly two dozen states have had to take similar benefits haircuts over the last decade.

And when Senator Dominguez found yet another

opportunity to cast doubt upon the HRA, I have to ask where this concern has been during the past eighteen months of the campaign? Are there any *other* programs he suddenly disapproves of, and might move against as president?

Finally, I think his little "genius academy" idea is great—although it might already exist. It's called the wonderful American public school system! Where children of all races and economic backgrounds get the best education the world has to offer. Senator, if you want to privately fund this pet project, be my guest. But don't tangle the practical concept of UBI with your unspoken prejudice against our schools and their thousands of wonderful teachers.

Dominguez: Madam President, I have to hand it to you. Not only are you able to draw out my deepest secrets, you then twist my words so you can pander to the bloated teachers unions—many of which took a hit to their own pensions, I might add.

But wait, please! Let me continue. The fact of the matter is that our approach to education has been obsolete for decades. If you want to keep the elementary and university systems intact, fine. But my goodness, study after study points to the fact that imprisoning our adolescents and teenagers in the upper-middle and high school grades is perhaps the biggest cause of dysfunction, repression, crime, and unfulfilled potential across the country.

If we want any chance of keeping pace within this perpetually disruptive economy, as well as competing with other countries, for heaven's sake, unshackle our students from grades eight through twelve. They're already learning about what interests them on their phones, so why not—instead of just letting them roam free, as I'm sure the president would accuse me of advocating—offer apprenticeship tracks, so that these kids can learn the ultimate skill of focus? That crucial ability can then be applied to any number of passions after the apprenticeship ends.

Jeffries-Lao: May I get in a few words?

Hauer: Quickly, please.

Jeffries-Lao: Thank you. If this is all so important to my opponent, why has he never presented legislation of this kind in the Senate? I need not mention that his three children attend private school.

Dominguez: As did your daughter.

Hauer: Mine too, if that helps either of you score points. ... Madam President, so far we've mostly talked about the HRA and other issues in terms of the big picture, government entities and whatnot. But at the end of the day, this all boils down to real people. To use a rather crude but popular phrase, what do you say to Americans who right now are glaring at each other from opposite sides of the spreadsheet?

Jeffries-Lao: I want all Americans to know that I understand if they're feeling frustrated. If you're a Beneficiary, maybe things in your neighborhood haven't started to turn around yet. And to Debtors struggling to find a job but still forced to pay into the program, I truly sympathize. While I support the HRA's mission with all my heart, I'm not among those fringe groups that see it as a hammer of retribution. Reparations means restitution. Nothing more, nothing less. If exploring ways to help Debtors bridge the gap makes sense, perhaps my opponent can draft legislation to this effect when he's back in the Senate next January.

Dominguez: You've got to admire the president's confidence. In the six days since the Sentinels of Jubilee's second broadcast, we've seen demonstrations in thirty cities. Congress has received tens of thousands of phone calls from citizens who are scared about the safety of their personal data, as well as their children's future under a program which, in all honesty, now seems destined for failure.

With the election still weeks away, we've just seen how a lot can happen very quickly. Maybe you'll soon discover that I, and not the incumbent, am the right person for the job.

Jeffries-Lao: That was quite the cryptic remark, Victor. Does the senator from Arizona know something that the rest of us don't?

Dominguez: If I did, it would only be the latest in a succession of surprises that keep blindsiding this administration.

Hauer: I'm going to jump in here and stop you both before things get really ugly. It's time for closing statements, sixty seconds each. Senator Dominguez, you have the floor.

Dominguez: When my family came to this country fifty-eight years ago, the landscape was different in so many ways. Still, the bedrock American values of hard work, faith, and family remain. But it is now clear to me, that the founding of the HRA may very well have started a cascade of unintended consequences that pose unknown dangers to us all. Instead of harmony, we see a conflict brewing between people bent on revenge and those who nurse resentment in their hearts. The prospect of this bad blood getting out of hand could be disastrous for everyone.

When you vote for me on November seventh, you're telling Washington that you demand a more sensible policy when wielding this or any other bureaucracy. Because the stability of our nation may depend on it. And giving our children a chance to fly without tethers demands it.

Hauer: And now to you, President Jeffries-Lao.

Jeffries-Lao: I could, but I won't stoop to telling some heartfelt family anecdote in hopes of scoring cheap points. My record—first as a school board member, then as a state representative, and finally as a governor—is what put me in the White House. And it is your belief in my ability to succeed, despite all obstacles put in my way, which will send me back to Washington with a mandate not to let up, not to take my foot off the accelerator—and to fulfill the HRA's mission! Thank you, good night, and may God bless the United States of America!

Hauer: This concludes the third and final presidential debate of the 2028 campaign. Thank you both, President Eileen Jeffries-Lao and Senator Victor Dominguez. And we'll see you at the polls on November seventh. For MBC News, I'm Tad Hauer saying good night.

5. THE DISCOVERY

Kate Donohugh had taken TJ's advice and stayed away from work. Not only that, she didn't go back home to Brooklyn at all.

She tried her best to explain to Chris why she needed some time alone, and if she sounded unconvincing, it would be fair to say that Kate also didn't fully understand the reasons. But she believed everything that had happened to her this year was for a reason, so she had no choice but to follow the thread and discover what life was trying to tell her.

Kate especially wanted to prove the Sentinels' masked speaker wrong for suggesting that she had been brainwashed. She thought that revisiting the site of her political awakening might be a sensible place to start investigating—meaning that she'd have to make her way from South Dakota to Boston.

The hospital where she was staying slowly drained of its mobs of law enforcement, government bureaucrats, and *DDM TV* fans now that Luis Ortega had woken up. He too would soon return home to Los

Angeles after passing some final medical tests.

Kate was told that she was free to take one of the charter flights headed back to New York, but then would be on her own getting to Boston. By chance while passing through a lobby packed with media, she recognized one camera crew's call letters as being from Boston and asked them if she might catch whatever flight they were taking home.

Some negotiations followed, with Kate ultimately agreeing to give the reporter an exclusive one-on-one interview in exchange for the ride. To her relief the questions were mostly softball, and she arrived in Boston on Saturday evening feeling like she'd taken one small step toward PR redemption.

The first thing she did was meet up with several old friends from college. They sang the night away at a karaoke bar, then ate brunch the following morning. A wave of bottomless mimosas helped to wash away the worst of Kate's South Dakota-induced anxiety, and after leaving the restaurant she felt ready to begin her quest.

She first planned to spend the afternoon quietly reminiscing on the Boston University campus, breathing in the crisp fall air as she strolled among the trees and old brick buildings, before sitting in on some classes the next day in hopes of gaining insight into her past. But when she arrived, Kate came upon a chaotic scene that was nothing like what she had envisioned.

Thousands of people were gathered in the common areas and marching around the walkways in support of the HRA. Speakers with bullhorns cursed the Sentinels of Jubilee while railing in defense of Beneficiary rights.

There were wild costumes and manic dance circles. Other people held up signs with messages such as

"Free MARVIN," "Our Debt is a Badge of Honor," "United Cat Ladies of Non-England," and "Come On, Eileen!" And somewhere in the crowd a group was chanting, "Hey, hey, ho, ho, the SOJ has got to go!"

One of the speakers, a gangly white man in his late twenties decked out in jean vest and candy-striped pants, very much resembled Bjorn, the first guy Kate seriously dated after joining the world of activism. Bjorn had come from a well-to-do family, did the social justice circuit for ten years, then bowed out to fall back on his roots. The last Kate had heard, he was married with two kids and worked at a private law firm in St. Louis.

Today's speaker was riling up the audience with wild fist pumps.

"...and of course the scourge of whiteness," he was saying. "As if a devilish philosophy which operated virtually unchecked for hundreds of years would just roll over in one night. Ha! Who were we kidding? We really shouldn't be surprised that these so-called Jubileers would try to bring down the program that's finally delivering long-overdue Reparations.

"So you can't run and hide! You've got to stand up and fight back in this almighty tug-of-war for power. Because right now it's five hundred years to three. We've still got a lot of work to do to make things right. And that's why we've gathered here today—to rise up in solidarity! People of all shades, genders, and backgrounds coming together to fight for equity, to fight for the HRA, and of course, to ensure the re-election of our greatest champion, Eileen Jeffries-Lao..."

Kate walked on. At one point her path was blocked by several weeping students who were rolling around on the ground. Above them stood a weathered man in

Tribal shaman costume who somberly waved a smoking branch while praising the spirit of "Soaring MARVIN." Kate worked her way around this piece of performance art and came upon a beret-wearing Latiza dressed in all black who was giving an impassioned speech.

"We tried to do it their way," she said. "Some might even say the right way. But it didn't take long for Debtors to sabotage the program. Should we really trust these Sentinels to honor their word? I say no! Should we believe that this presidential administration, which allowed the HRA to get so blindsided in the first place, is up to the task of fixing this mess? Again, I say no!

"So what can we do? What we must! There are still millions of documents out there that need to be scanned. And billions, if not trillions of dollars that still need to be turned over to their rightful inheritors. But hear me out, because I'm not calling for any kind of direct violence. We don't want all those trigger-happy NRA types to start shooting us from the bushes, now do we? We've got to be smart, just like those Sentinels.

"Tragically, the ballot box wasn't enough. But the bullet will only get a lot of us killed. We've got to create a new vision for what the word 'revolution' means in the twenty-first century. So please, join us for discussions on the commons every afternoon between now and the election. We at the Future Dream Collective have no choice but to go back to the drawing board to find a way to assert our voices with power, should the unthinkable happen and we enter a post-Reparations world.

"You still don't think it could happen? I'm sorry, but Victor Dominguez is a Latizo-in-name-only. We all know that as president he'd side with the anti-HRA forces and shut it down. So you see, we're backed into a corner with no true advocates to rely on anymore. Win or lose in this election, the responsibility rests on our shoulders to take back what is rightfully ours. Are you ready to forge Reparations 2.0?"

The crowd roared its approval. Kate kept moving. She looked over the tables covered with political pamphlets and literature. This was the type of gathering she'd been to a hundred times before—but today she just couldn't get into it. Instead she felt numbly distant from these HRA allies who, if they'd noticed her, would surely have commiserated and offered her words of encouragement.

But the instant Kate realized that it was very likely someone in this crowd would recognize her, she wanted to be as far away as possible. She did *not* have the strength to be thrust forward again and have to give any sort of speech.

Kate hastily bought a Che Guevara scarf from one of the vendors and tied it over her head, then hunched forward and slowly pushed her way through the mass of bodies. At last she got free and hurried away. She took one last look back at the spectacle and felt torn by the mixed emotions of apathy, pride, and dread.

Afterwards, she simply could not see herself going back to attend any lectures. What she really needed was a break from everything.

Kate called her parents down in Northern Virginia and asked if she could stay with them. This proved to be exactly what she needed—to fall into the arms of their unconditional love within the comfort of her childhood home. Just a few days spent marinating in this rejuvenating elixir refreshed Kate so much that, on a whim, she decided to reach out to her beloved former principal Mrs. Olney and see if she might be allowed to visit the school. The woman was delighted to hear from such a distinguished alumnus and insisted upon escorting her around personally.

So it was on Thursday, exactly one week after her whirlwind flight to South Dakota and the subsequent Sentinels of Jubilee broadcast, that Kate arrived at Washington-McKinley High School in Arlington.

She buzzed at the armor-plated front entrance, then gave her credentials and leaned in for a retinal scan. The door swung open and a police officer in full tactical gear waved her in. He silently led her from the lobby into a side hallway, with eyes alert and one hand resting on a hip holster.

"Oh, hello there, Kate!"

A woman in bright red pantsuit had popped out of a nearby doorway and was approaching quickly. The officer peeled away without a sound.

"My goodness, look at you. All grown up!"

"Thank you, Mrs. Olney. You don't look a day older than at my graduation."

"Why, thank you. The kids keep us on our toes, and I guess that makes me feel young."

"I do remember some of us being little terrors, myself excluded of course."

"I'm sure of it. Now, you said on the phone that you were trying to solve a mystery. What exactly is the problem, and how can I help? Please, sit down."

They had entered a private office past the reception desk and now took their seats.

"You see," Kate began, "I've been trying to track down where the 'me' that you see today came from. Where that all began."

"I don't quite follow. Surely you're a collection of your family, your classmates, life experiences, and—if we did our jobs—maybe you remember some of us as more than just regurgitators of textbook lessons."

"Of course! That's exactly why I'm here, in fact. My high school years were wonderful, but I have to admit that not long after going away to college, I began a bit of a wild streak. Maybe even using politics as a cover for partying, at least in the beginning before I got serious about activism."

"Oh, that tends to happen when you're on your own for the first time. We do our best to provide a controlled environment here. Help shelter children as long as possible from the bad influences that might derail them. But please, go on."

"Well, after you put it like that, I don't really know what more to ask."

"No bother then. But let me give you a little tour of the building since you've come all the way back here. Maybe it will jump-start your mind."

"That would be lovely. I'm curious to see if our field hockey team record of most goals in a season still stands."

They got up and exited through reception. Mrs. Olney first took Kate past the trophy case, then said, "So much has changed since you were here fifteen years ago. Once we were able to drop the name Lee, that's when things really started progressing."

"I remember hearing about that name change."

"Seemed only fitting to replace him with President McKinley, haha. Anyway, since we're about to pass the gymnasium, I'll show you the ingenious little setup we have there. To encourage physical activity among these digital monsters, we've got VR headsets programmed with all kinds of games to get the kids moving."

Kate watched as thirty students in yellow spandex suits jumped and ran and flashed their hands across a large open area while participating in both solo and group virtual sports. One girl, who was walking directly toward them, stopped abruptly and threw one arm up high with a big smile, then after several seconds lowered her arm and strutted away.

"Drum majorette," Olney said. "I'm surprised the software's still in there considering that we ended the football program back in 'twenty-four. For safety reasons, of course."

Kate next followed the principal across the main foyer into the library.

Olney said, "I'm so excited for you to see this! The kids, with the help of local HRA liaisons, have taken it upon themselves to add our collection to MARVIN's pipeline. Look, right there."

She pointed to a chrome HRA scanner that was in a corner rotunda. One student fed papers into its left-side collection port, while another sat at a nearby table slicing the binding off of a book.

"Volunteers," Olney said. "They get extra credit for helping upload these volumes. Working their way forward from oldest to newest."

Kate nodded. "I'm surprised you still have so many books made of actual paper. Will they recycle the ones they're scanning in right now?"

"Oh, no. We have a fancy machine that rebinds them, then it's back onto the shelf. You can't be too careful about keeping extra copies around, because you never know what one day might be considered an inconvenient archive—especially now! But pardon my…"

"It's fine, Mrs. Olney. You're doing a wonderful job here. What else can you show me?"

"Well… Do you remember the art teacher Ms. Herron? She's a bit of a star in her own right around here."

"Of course I do! She was a real task master, but we all excelled under her guidance."

"Indeed. She's still here whipping her little army into shape. Let's drop in on her class and see what they're up to."

Kate and Mrs. Olney slipped into the back of a classroom that was dark except for a large LED screen at the front, and a small lamp on the lectern nearby.

"All art, like all ideas," the woman leading the class said, "is a weapon. But within each warhead is a seed. Because why go into battle and achieve victory if you end up leaving the land barren?"

The image of a hand holding a paintbrush appeared on the screen.

"This—and not a gun—is the most powerful weapon a person can wield. Why? Because the gun can only strike fear, coerce behavior, and kill. But the implement of artistic expression is a more subtle conqueror. As subjective ideas enter the minds of the target audience, each hair of the paintbrush snakes its way through their psyche, cleaning out the old beliefs and leaving fresh new concepts in their place.

"What? You don't believe that something as innocent as a painted canvas could be used to manipulate, redirect, or demoralize a population? Allow me!"

The next image to appear was a news website screen capture of an article titled "Modern Art was CIA 'Weapon'."

"Look at that right there. *The Independent* out of England, dated October of 1995. This article was the first to reveal—or admit—how throughout the Cold War, our own government funded the Modern Art movement to counter Soviet propaganda. But of course, our own people were exposed to these works as well.

"Now, consider the change that occurred in art from one century to the next. Look at these magnificent nineteenth century landscapes of the American wilderness. Some of these massive paintings are fifteen feet tall and twenty feet wide! Notice the attention to detail in every tree. They are masterpieces of realism!

"Compare that technique with the twentieth century works of Jackson Pollack. Utter devolution! A child, or a horse kicking over a bucket of paint, could achieve similar results. Yet Pollack's works were promoted around the world—and as we now know, not due to merit alone, but also by the hidden hand."

A sequence of movie posters and pop culture images cycled through the screen as Herron continued. "So you see, it's everywhere. In all forms of art. The world war for your mind. Where the directors are the generals, the studios are the munitions factories, and the actors serve in the infantry. And for a long time— until about thirty years ago, when high-speed internet and digital cameras eliminated the need for costly materials—until then, we were all at the mercy of what the centralized powers wanted to show us. They told us not just what to believe, but even what to think about.

"Here is an article documenting how our own Pentagon has provided production assistance and made script recommendations for hundreds of TV shows and films. This is why, when people go on about the separation of church and state, I retort by saying that we should also keep the government's hands off of the arts.

"But when you realize that all art is political, you understand that governments are just trying to win the game. And therefore *you* have to play by those rules too."

A photograph of a mirror appeared on screen.

"Yes, you. The days of painting for enjoyment, or

sculpting merely to bring something aesthetically pleasing into existence, are over. Why? Because you are the change agents in a war where the fate of the world is at stake. I know it seems like a heavy burden, but you should be thankful that you can do your part simply by using an illustration program on your computer. Would you rather be carrying a rifle and a hundred pounds of gear through some jungle? Thankfully, you *don't* have to kill anybody—only bad ideas.

"Now, normally I would say that in turn, nobody is trying to kill you. But after all that has happened in the past couple weeks with these Sentinels of Jubilee hackers, I fear that we may really have to fight to protect all the progress we've made this decade.

"So we as artists must use our vision to ensure that at the end of the day, a government program is not all we rely upon to determine the success or failure of our philosophy. It takes changing hearts, minds, and even pigment to achieve lasting victory. So everyone, grab the paint cans which I have set out on your tables, and join me as we fulfill the promise of the revolution!"

The screen came alive with a sensual cinematic tribal ritual. Percussive dance music played as scantily clad bodies writhed against each other in torchlight. Ms. Herron raised a toddler's plastic pool above her head triumphantly, then placed it below the screen and beckoned her students forward.

One by one, silhouettes rose from their seats and approached, pouring quarts of paint into the pool while their teacher danced and swayed, stirring the different colors together with an enormous wooden spoon.

"Oh, yes!" she moaned. "The future is ours! Blend, blend, my precious proteges. Dump it all in and stir, stir them together. Oh, Keanu…"

Kate waited in the hallway while Ms. Herron cleaned herself up after the class ended. The paint ritual had gotten a little out of hand when she'd fallen into the pool and almost pulled a nearby female student in along with her. As the kids walked past her, Kate noticed how young they all looked. *These are some heavy ideas to be putting in their heads,* she thought.

But Kate and her classmates had sat through similar lectures back in her day, though perhaps not with the same wild theatrics. And there had been other teachers that were as passionate about the underlying philosophies of life as they were regarding the actual subjects being taught.

"A pan-comprehensive curriculum facilitates a fully integrated, trans-hierarchical society," Kate remembered one world history teacher as having said —or something to that effect. It sometimes took so many hyphenated slogans to encapsulate the whole progressive message, that even Kate had to smile while trying to keep up with it all. *Well, as long as one's heart is in the right place...*

The classroom door opened and out stepped Ms. Herron in all her glory: the large head of flat-topped, pepper-gray hair, thick-toothed smile behind burgundy lips, and green eyes made vivid by thick black eyeliner.

"Katie, oh my God! Did you just see all that?"

Kate gave her a hug and said, "It's so great to see you. It looks like you haven't lost a step in all these years."

"Shush! How old do you think I am? And anyway, you know me. An undulating priestess gathers no moss! So, what brings the world famous Kate Francis —excuse me, Donohugh—back to our hallowed halls?"

As they began to walk toward the teachers' lounge, Kate said, "Since I gather from the lecture that you're familiar with what's happened to the HRA, I'll get right to the point. Honestly, this whole situation has knocked me way off balance."

"How so?" Herron asked.

"I mean, I've talked about this with my husband, and had plenty of time on the plane to think as well, but I just can't shake the doubts and get back to work. So I don't know what I'm doing—searching for answers, or maybe some sort of affirmation that I'm really okay."

Herron motioned for Kate to enter the lounge. "Ah, so you've come back here as part of your journey. How fun! What's the verdict so far?"

Kate sat at a round table while Herron prepared coffees at the counter.

"On the surface," Kate said, "everything seems fine. Mrs. Olney even showed me how the kids in the library have bought into our mission and are scanning away."

"Mm-hmm."

"And you. Still a legend at taking seemingly random data, then synthesizing it into powerful ideas for the kids to digest and create new connections of their own—"

"Just like the warhead I speak of in my lectures," Herron said. "A plow clearing away the detritus in their minds, then planting new ideas in the ripe, freshly turned soil. Ah, yes…"

"But what if," Kate said, slowly stirring her coffee, "what if your students aren't quite ready at that age to have their minds blown?"

"They seem perfectly mature to me. Especially considering how much data they all consume pretty much from day one."

"But is it your place to sweep away everything

they've been taught up until now? Say, by their parents or earlier schooling? Don't you worry that these ideas might send them down a path that they otherwise would never have taken?"

"But it was always there," Herron said with a wave. "I just held up a lantern at the entrance to, let's say, promote awareness of the path's existence. And besides, these kids I teach have had other art teachers before me. Think back to learning the basics of drawing and painting in the early grades. They were planting seeds too. About how to see the world, what art does to people. On and on…"

"Maybe so," Kate said, "but is anyone mentally equipped at age fifteen to make such a momentous, perhaps irrevocable decision? I mean, one day they're just trying to figure out trigonometry, or their raging hormones, and then boom—a teacher anoints them, not simply as future leaders, but as change agents. That's quite a responsibility to be assigned out of the blue."

"My goodness, Kate. Haven't you been living the bold life of an advocate for many years now? Has it not been the most fulfilling ride to see your good deeds reverberate throughout the world?"

"Ms. Herron, you know I have. And with more impact than most. But who authorized me to change the world? What qualifies me to impose my political views onto others?"

"If *you* aren't qualified to lead and help the less fortunate, then I truly don't know who is."

"I'm certainly able to do it now, but that wasn't always the case. It's as if one day at college a switch just flipped. Suddenly my mind activated into this persona that on the surface embraced progressive values, but underneath was more like a robot. Reciting the programmed catch phrases, doing all the right activities, and even wearing a sort of group-approved uniform. But what if I never actually wanted to do any of that?"

Kate felt her eyes well up and looked down in embarrassment.

"Now, now," Herron said. "It's okay to self-analyze, but you're already in pretty deep, Kate. What else would you do? Leave all the Beneficiaries on the side of the road to fend for themselves while you go pop out a bunch of kids? Ah, yes, the old cop-out and pop-out…"

Herron chuckled to herself and toyed with the lip of her coffee mug.

"You never had children of your own, right?" Kate asked.

"No, all of you are my legacy. My sacred crops, exported around the world, each year spreading these fruitful ideas far and wide."

"And do many of us come back to visit you?"

"Oh, some do," Herron said. "Now and again. But the important thing is that they're out there doing the good work. Look at you, for example. I couldn't be any prouder than seeing what a force you've become for the HRA—and especially in knowing that I played a hand in stirring up that inner fire that has driven you this whole time."

Kate brought a hand to her forehead.

She said, "And I have marched all these miles for you obediently. To think that I entered your classroom hoping to gain an appreciation for art, and maybe to learn how to sketch… But I walked out of there as part of a sleeper cell, just waiting for my mission at some future date."

"Hmph!" Herron bristled. "I always stated it explicitly: All politics is war. All art is political.

Therefore all art is a weapon of war. Don't wilt now at the first sight of your own blood. And please don't act as if you were fooled or betrayed."

"But the young mind sees these things as a kind of performance," Kate said. "Or hyperbole, at least. We're all taking in so much information about life and the world during those years. It should all just blend in, like your paints. But with teachers like you, something else lingered... took root... and it never left."

"Yes! That was my seed! I've been trying to tell you that the whole time. Forget the artists, forget the paintings. This war is a *dream* responsibility, an *honor* to fight in. How dare you get us so close to victory, and now think about bowing out or undermining the mission just because you took a little shrapnel on live TV. You want a Purple Heart for your trouble? Fine! But really, you should be thankful to end up stacked in an unmarked mass grave, if in your dying moment you know that your life was given to win the sacred War for Equity."

Kate began to shiver. She rose from the chair and absently slung her handbag over her shoulder.

"Thank you, Ms. Herron," she said softly. "Your words have been very instructive. I think I'll go home now."

She moved toward the doorway and Herron stood up behind her.

The woman said, "Get back out there, Corporal Donohugh, and make us all proud. Hail victory... Hail equity..."

Kate crept out of the lounge and slunk down the hallway as the woman's cackles echoed behind her. A soothing series of notes chimed, then a torrent of students poured into the space around her. She looked at their young faces, so bright and hopeful with shining eyes, then ran into a bathroom and sobbed in a stall.

After she got herself under control, Kate left the school building and walked to a nearby grassy area with picnic tables. She sat down under a tree and closed her eyes. Her mind was numb. She looked up and watched the rays of sunshine twinkling through the branches and leaves onto the ground beside her. She thought of the masked man's own dazzling neon blue eyes.

"You were right," she whispered. "I was brainwashed. They got inside all of our minds. But now what am I supposed to do?"

6. HOMETOWN HERO

Myra Jenkins spread a dozen vibrant fabric swatches across the tabletop that was next to an opaque glass window. One by one, she held them up against the warm yellow light that came through, then made notes on a pad.

She narrowed the swatches down to three and set the others aside. Next she pulled a tape measure from her hip and took several measurements around the window, then added to her notes.

A few minutes later, another black woman who was older than her entered the room and said, "Well, Myra, how are things going in here?"

"Hi, Ms. Wallace. I got the measurements for the windows right here. And I picked out a few color samples that I liked."

"Oh, let me see those."

Myra fanned out the swatches for Ms. Wallace, then held each one up. "See, it looks good with the daylight. Plus with these kind of beige floors, I don't know, they all just sort of fit together."

"Interesting. Now, of the three, which is your favorite?"

"Oh, I don't know."

"Come on, I want your opinion. You've already done such a good job redecorating the daycare and the lobby."

"Okay then. Thank you. At first I wanted the mint green, but then the big desk over there caught my eye. That gray, it's really dark. And when I hold up this color…"

"Wow, I see! It's very striking."

"Yeah. The royal blue makes everything come alive, but the room still seems serious. I don't think the green says 'work' like this one does."

Ms. Wallace took the blue swatch from Myra and set it on the desk. "Then it's settled. I'll have Edgar double-check your measurements—if you don't mind—and then we'll place the order."

"Oh, thank you, Ms. Wallace. This is all so fun. I never expected to be doing anything this exciting when I started working down in the daycare."

"Well, I'm just sorry these HRA trade schools lean so heavily on training people for brute blue-collar jobs. I wish we offered art classes too."

"That would be nice. I've almost got my GED done though, so this place isn't all bad."

"And who knows? After you get that diploma and do a few more of these projects, maybe your portfolio will be big enough to apply to a professional interior design program."

"Yes, ma'am. I appreciate you giving me this chance to help out."

"Of course, Myra. Give your baby girl a kiss for me now."

"I will, thank you."

Myra went into the ladies room and pulled out her phone. She scrolled to the pictures of the other rooms she had redecorated, and then envisioned how this new space would look after the curtains were installed. She smiled, then washed her hands and walked down to the daycare.

After the evening shift arrived at five-thirty, Myra clocked out and bundled up baby Sarah. As soon as they reached the sidewalk in front of the school, a sparkling crimson Buick tooted its horn and pulled up from down the block.

The engine turned off and out stepped a tall, lean man wearing a leather trench coat and white skull-cap. "Wassup, baby?" he said with a little smile.

"Right on time, Octavius. Thank you."

"Oh, you know. Only the best transportation for the most beautiful girl in the world."

"You don't have to say that…"

"I'm talkin' about my daughter. Come here, little thing."

Octavius carefully took Sarah in his arms and placed a kiss on the child's pink beanie. Myra flipped the passenger seat forward and watched as he tenderly placed the infant into the rear car seat.

Octavius double-checked the belt fasteners, then said, "Okay, where to?"

"Home."

"You ain't hungry?"

"Mama's probably cooking something already. She loves that new kitchen. I can't believe what's got into her!"

"I'm starving," Octavius said as he revved the engine. "Let's hope she made something good!"

When they entered the condo a short while later, Octavius rubbed his hands together. "Oh, Mizz

Jenkins? Something smells delicious in here. What are you cooking up for me?"

"Actually," a woman of about forty said, "I have a real surprise for both of you."

Just then, Clyde stepped out of the kitchen wearing an apron and holding up a spatula.

"Hey guys," he said with a playful lisp. "Celebrity chef here just sharing some recipes."

"My man!" Octavius said.

Myra set Sarah down in a highchair and gave Clyde a big hug.

"Hi, little brother. It's so good to see you. We love this place so much."

"Nah, forget about it. Y'all is my motivation, my inspiration."

Ms. Jenkins picked up her phone and said, "Squeeze in together. Let me get a look at you two. I'm so proud..."

While she snapped a few pictures, Octavius dropped his coat onto a chairback and moved into the living room. He sat down in the recliner and started flipping through a magazine.

"Hey," Clyde called out, "y'all didn't pick up Tee?"

"He's fine," Myra said. "This neighborhood is way better than the old place we stayed."

"Hey now," Octavius muttered.

Clyde put his arm around Myra. "It may be nice, but we ain't that far down the road from all that. I don't want him running around in the dark. He still too young."

"Alright, Uncle Clyde," Ms. Jenkins said. "You've let your voice be heard. Just wait til he gets home. The look that's gonna be on his face..."

Myra stepped into the kitchen and started preparing Sarah's bottle. She said, "So Mister DJ, tell us what's been going on this week."

Clyde took a bag of popcorn off the counter and threw a piece into his mouth. "Doing that frequent flyer thing, you know. Left LA about a week ago before heading over to—"

"Oh, how did that all go?"

"I got the royal treatment, so I can't complain too bad. The fans came out to the club for autographs and pictures. But check this out—that agent dude say he could set me up with Bekki Triage."

"Ooh," Ms. Jenkins said, "that girl is fine! Got them Indian princess eyes. Watch out!"

"Haha, I know. But they smooth out there in Cali. Pitch you a real nice deal—big money, big booties—hoping you don't see the strings attached."

"But Clyde, how much are they offering?"

"A lot. But it ain't just about the money. They kinda takin' control. Not just of what you do, but who you are. It's crazy how deep they think about this stuff and plan it all out."

"They gonna let you sing, dance, see the world? You want to go to Japan, right?"

"Of course, Mama."

"So why you playing hard to get? I know a lot of other people who can sing good, and ain't nobody knocking down their door to put them up on stage."

"I know, I know. I'm just thinking on it. Because I sign, and that's it. Locked in. I did run it by Nolan a little bit. He said to sit on it for a while. Says if they really want me, they'll reach out again."

"You better listen to what he says, then. God bless that Mr. Simmons," Ms. Jenkins said with a sigh.

Myra turned and gave her a look. "Oh, you like him now?"

"Give your mama a break. I don't know about all

that business stuff. I was just looking out for my baby boy. Glad we got ours. Got mouths to feed around here."

"Yeah, well," Clyde said, "Nolan's always treated me right. Even back when we was doin' the little jobs, like catching drones for a few bucks. And also now, when we selling my track in the hundreds of thousands."

"Believe me, I am so thankful that this miracle helped get us out of the poorhouse. But I just want to make sure we covered."

"Mama, you got to chill," Myra said. "Most of that legal stuff is done by computers anyway. All the downloads, the money… Even the taxes he got to pay."

"Oh, look at you now, Miss GED. Take a couple classes and you think you know everything. But it don't take an accountant to know how human nature is. Trust is a nice idea, but I guess I've been burned too many times to feel comfortable like y'all do. Especially now that they got him paying *in* to the system."

Clyde said, "There's all these contracts out there already written up. Business, music, whatever. You just got to pick the right one."

"But what the hell's in them? How do you know someone ain't trying to pull a fast one on you?"

"Mama, thank you for watching out for me. But it's a new world out there. Everything is done on a public spreadsheet."

"Oh Lord, not another spreadsheet! That's what the HRA uses and look at the mess they're in."

"Hey, I got a new song for y'all. 'Fight the spreadsheet! Yeah, yeah. We got to… fight… fight the spreadsheet!' What you think?"

"Aw, you playin'. But that's okay. I hope you don't send that one to the agent, though. He'll delete your number!"

Clyde threw his arm around her shoulders and they all laughed.

Just then the front door opened. Tyrell walked in carrying a bookbag and a tiny football. His face lit up. "Uncle Clyde!" He ran over and jumped into Clyde's arms.

"How you do, little man?"

"I'm good. I like my new bedroom."

"Oh, you do? Finally got it all set up?"

"Yeah. It's quiet. I can't hear the people next door no more."

"That's good, real good. And how school going?"

"It's okay."

"What they teaching you now? Math? Science?"

"Kind of. The teacher put on some goggles. Then she held up this glass, and it had red stuff inside. I don't always know what she doin', though."

"That's okay. Keep at it. You'll learn things by, what they call it... Osmosis!"

"Yeah! She said that word one time."

"What about PE? They got you playing any sports?"

"Naw. But we get to go outside for recess."

"Oh yeah? What you do out there? We need to get your jump shot dialed in while you still young."

"We got a new game called 'gotcha'. All the kids get in on it."

"How it go?"

"Like, everyone at school got a tablet. If you see another kid doing something bad, you put it in there."

"I don't follow. How you mean?"

"Other day, I saw this white girl calling this white boy all these names. So I start recording all that. And when that boy cried and went away, I sent that video over."

"Wait. What?"

"Yeah, so next time we at recess, this older boy Alberto, he take out his tablet and see what in there. Then all the kids who did bad stuff got to get punished."

Clyde looked around the room. "Are y'all hearing this?"

Myra shrugged her shoulders. "Kids get up to all kinds of silly stuff. You ain't no angel, neither."

"Go on, Tee," Clyde said.

"Alberto yell out that we got to have a Revenge Event. You know, 'cause you been hittin' or stealin' from other kids."

"So what happens?"

"Whatever you did gets done back to you. 'With interest,' Alberto say. By everybody."

"Even the black kids are taking lumps?"

"Yeah. Anyone who got caught. It don't matter they color."

"And you been taking part in these Revenge Events?"

"You got to. Last week, we all put milk on this boy's head. 'Cause he tried stealing a drink from this girl. But someone got it on tape, so…"

"So you did that? And that was fun?"

"Seein' that milk go down his face, like, we laughed and laughed! But today they got me. It wasn't no fun."

"What happened? What the hell they do to you?"

"I got bit."

"What?! Where?"

"They all got me on the leg. See, one time I bit this other girl…"

Clyde reached down and rolled up Tyrell's pant leg. He slapped his forehead when he saw a dozen small bite impressions all over the boy's calf and ankle. Myra rushed over. "Oh, my goodness…" she said.

Ms. Jenkins leaned over the sink and started muttering. "And this was supposed to be the good school!"

"Well, he ain't cut. He ain't bleeding." Myra rolled the pant leg back down.

Clyde was pacing back and forth. He said to Tyrell, "So they having little trials at school? Who's watching you during all this? Or are you kids doing it when nobody around?"

"First it was just us, but now a couple teachers help it go."

"So they got y'all spyin' and snitchin' on each other, huh? These are your classmates, your friends. This is no good. Real-time Reparations. For kids! Is this what people want? Getting the next generation working against each other, even before they understand why it was all set up? This ain't right. Tee, next time they try to make you play, you tell 'em no."

"But what if they say it's my turn? If you caught, you caught."

"You tell them your Uncle Clyde said it has to stop. Make 'em do jumping jacks or plant a damn tree instead."

Myra said, "Clyde, you're right. I had no idea they was being so rough to each other. He just kept talkin' about this fun game gotcha, but he never explained it like that before. I'm gonna talk to the school first thing tomorrow when we drop him off. Ain't that right, Octavius?"

Octavius had come in from the living room while Tyrell told his story, and now had a sour expression on his face. "No doubt," he said. "I'll back you up. But don't make me talk too much, or I'll get us all in trouble."

"No, I just want you by my side. Alright, Tee, let's get you ready for dinner."

As Myra took Tyrell upstairs and Ms. Jenkins returned to the stove, Clyde leaned toward Octavius and said quietly, "Hey, can I get a private word with you for a few?"

"Of course. Where you want to talk?"

"Let's move to the garage, shoot some pool."

Clyde set the rack while Octavius got himself a beer from the fridge.

"So what's on your mind?" Octavius said.

Clyde picked up a cue, looking at the tip intently while he applied chalk. "I see you been coming around more often lately."

"Oh, you know."

"I'm glad, is what I'm saying. I don't need you to explain your reasons."

"I do what I do. You do what you do. That's what's up."

"It's all good. We family. And, I want to keep it in the family. 'Cause money's only just one part of it."

"Money come. Money go. And that's how it goes." Octavius took a swig of beer.

"Yeah. It's just been crazy for everyone the past couple months. And you know, I look up to you. So I don't want all this DJC stuff to make things awkward."

"Clyde, I respect what you did for your sister. You did good getting her set up in a nicer place. I know I looked out for you before, threw you some jobs now and again. But I ain't coming to this house looking for no handouts. I got a kid with your sister, and I'll keep doin' whatever it takes to provide for them."

"No doubt. I'll never forget you bringin' me that work, teachin' me the hustle. But you run in a rough world. It's too hot for me. And I ain't trying to step on your feet. It's just, we ain't got no dad, so with this money I got to look out for my mom and my nephew."

"Be crazy not to. And selfish."

"So I want to make sure we square. Because something magic happened with my song to make all this possible. I can't have no bad blood mess it up, now that we got it."

"Glad you coming at me with this direct. So keep going—what do you want?"

Clyde licked his lips.

"Right now Nolan's getting pulled away to other stuff. He's a star in his own way too, kinda. So I'll be fighting off the vultures without him. You's family— your daughter is my niece. So what I'm saying is... That world out there that loves me right now, and wants me to give them more... That's not your scene— they're not so hard on the outside, but they work on you in your mind. They try to twist you with words. But Octavius, I need a rock on my side. I know who you are. I know *what* you are. So I can trust you. And I'm asking, can I rely on you to be there? Watch my back?"

Octavius set his beer down on the pool table rail and looked Clyde dead in the eyes.

"I hear what you sayin'. I'm in this now. More than before, when it was just me and Myra. You and me, we in it together too. So what you need, protection?"

"Something like that. Call it hometown gristle. Man, those people out in LA, it's like they come from a different planet. Everyone acts kinda silly, like they putting on a show—but they ain't stupid. They always workin' you somehow. You know, distract you with something flashy, then boom! You under they wing. It kinda scared me. So that's why I'm coming at you with this. I need someone who can look at situations with street eyes. And teach me how to spot the angle quick!"

"No doubt. Your bullshit posse."

"Ha, yeah. Keep me out of their nets so I can keep doing what I do. Make music, touch people."

"Clyde, you got an innocent soul, boy. I don't know how this all gonna play out, but if you need me to watch out for you, I do it. You keep this DJC thing rolling—you know I always wanted that for you—and we both look after your sister. Then who knows… Maybe at the end of the day, I won't have to throw so many punches."

"Then relax one of them fists right now and shake my hand."

"My brutha."

"Family. Family, yo."

Clyde and Octavius joined hands and came together for a brief hug.

A moment later, Ms. Jenkins opened the door and called them in. Dinner was served.

7. MODESTIANITY

The dancers in blue skittered across the stage. Discordant notes from a cello sent them round and round wildly, until a violin's soothing melody won the day. The troupe eased into formation, with three men swaying gently on one side and being mirrored by three women across the stage. Standing motionless on a stool in the middle was an obscured figure wearing black.

Suddenly the groups ran toward each other, meeting and pairing off in an elegant spin. The silver glitter on their faces twinkled in the spotlight. The couples moved together rhythmically, exuding the sensuous without being sensual—they were as dignified as ballet, but with the exhilaration of a river flowing toward a waterfall.

The central figure spread its arms to reveal giant wings, then stepped down and approached one of the couples. With a wide swing of the arm, this bird-human cloaked them and then pirouetted away. The audience gasped when it saw that the pair had disappeared.

This mystery figure dispatched the other couples in

the same fashion, before bowing its head and closing the wings forward over its body. The stage lights cut to black and the crowd burst into applause. A moment later, the lights flashed back on and the entire cast of twenty dancers ran out and linked arms. The clapping continued for several minutes as the troupe took their bows.

One of the performers, a black man of medium complexion, gave a particularly vivid smile as he acknowledged the crowd. His journey to this moment had been even more unorthodox than the often unique life path that brought most people to the Mall of Absolution. And now he was on the cusp of moving one step closer to the inner circle of Modestianity.

The dancers waved and skipped away behind the curtain into the dressing room.

Bill Evans exchanged hugs with his fellow cast members before washing the makeup off his face. He then removed his costume and put on his blue teal robe, which was the standard uniform worn by all novitiates during the six-month trial period that followed their first commitment.

He exited the theater and found himself floating on air as he made his way back to the cloisters. Evening feast was approaching and he didn't want to be late, but when he saw that one of his mentors was giving a lecture in the courtyard, he sat down on the edge of a fountain to listen for a few moments.

"We are flesh-and-blood animals with wild energy," Brother Salazar said. "But in order to turn our passions into brilliance, we must not simply deny that they exist. Repression only leads to pathology. Thus, Modestianity is not the religion of prudery. We do not fear embracing the earthiness of the pagans. And if we are guilty of covering ourselves out of shame, it is only away from the heartless eyes of a technology that seeks to imprison the human spirit. But to our fellow humans, we are as open to the life cycle as the leaf that shines high above in springtime, and then journeys with the wind to enrich the soil elsewhere in death…"

Bill passed through the cloister's double doors just as a three-tone bell began to chime. He joined the stream of novitiates in hooded blue robes that flowed out from the bunk rooms into a dimly lit, wood-appointed dining hall.

Each man took a bowl from an end table, then shuffled forward as servers ladled out the portions of food. The men then sat down at several long tables and waited in silence. Someone thumped his utensil against the surface and said, "Let us be circumspect in our every deed."

"Amen," the group responded.

The men quietly discussed the events of their day. Some had taken food out to the refugees living in the surrounding parking lots and fields. Others had assisted in children's reading lessons.

The man sitting next to Bill nudged his arm. "What do you think—elder or kinsman?"

"Whatever the emissaries decide, I will accept," Bill replied.

"I hear they grill you pretty hard in there. Looking for your weaknesses."

"One final test to ensure we end up in the correct role, perhaps?"

"I had a lot of responsibility back in the real world. Don't want to be spinning my wheels with the kinsmen."

"Have patience, my brother. In light of all the refugees flooding our gates, it seems likely that the need for capable church members will also increase. If you don't advance to elder in tomorrow's ceremony, surely Mod will see to it that a vacancy or new post opens up for you soon."

"Mod, I hope you're right. Thanks for your ear, brother."

"It is an anxious time for us all. But also hopeful and exciting. Keep the faith."

The other man grumbled and poked at his food.

After feast, the men slowly filed across a walkway and entered a spacious open room which had a thin layer of blue carpeting that also ran up the wall several feet. They sat down on the floor and chatted quietly. A man wearing the blue-gray tunic and sash of an elder walked to the center of the space. He was followed by a kinsman in lighter gray who carried a transcription machine.

"Good evening," the elder said. "Mod be with you."

"And also with you," the group answered.

"On this Advancement Day eve, let us seek to remain focused on the work at hand. Every mapmaking session not only brings us closer to a deeper understanding of ourselves, but also contributes to the growing body of insights which will help guide mankind into a more balanced future. Whether lay member, novitiate, kinsman, elder, proponent, or emissary, everyone shares in the teachings as we refine our wisdom through questions and clarifications.

"So many of our brothers and sisters in the outside world have lost their way. Is that not proof that we will be needed, and that our work each night has value? Let us begin with Brother Fremont, whose letter to me provides tonight's first kernel. He says, 'My studies seem to reveal that serene poise is the key teaching. How can this be maintained when a) the church believes in certain immutable human traits, while b) the world itself changes at exponential rates?'

"A truly thoughtful paradox. Could it be that in having to grapple with so much external instability, we are forced to tap into powerful mental chambers that were previously unknown to us? While we do not *create* new human faculties, perhaps this process unlocks and strengthens capabilities that were simply dormant within. And because this world is ours, surely nothing that arises from it cannot be harnessed, fenced in, and steered to our purposes. Now, who is ready to divert the trail?"

An older man sitting against one of the walls stood up. "I would like to offer a small challenge."

"Very well, Brother Carmichael. Please…"

"What the year 2028 looks like would have been unimaginable to someone from 1928. Just as 1928 would stagger a person living in 1828. And yet man as a whole adapts step by step as time goes by. He does his best to weather displacement, while also taking advantage of the positive changes.

"But two thoughts trouble me now. First, what if new developments come so fast that no one is able to keep up? As if psychologically, we could not make the leap? Which leads to my greater fear. Will we reach a point where our creation is so intelligent and so self-sufficient, that not only does it not need us to maintain it, but it refuses to serve us?"

"Are you worried that one day AI will turn on us? Perhaps by killing or enslaving humanity?"

"It could be worse than that. What if the technology decides to abandon us? Turns its back, refuses to function at all, and leaves us out in the cold?"

The elder scratched his goatee while slowly moving across the room. "Yes, two very unsettling hypotheses. One hopes that the normal sputtering pace of human progress would negate the first idea. As for the other, would it be incorrect to infer that providing humans with everything they need is the real danger?

"Have we not already seen the cultural malaise of the past fifty years, as people living within this worldwide cargo cult have been divorced from the need to produce anything, as well as from the consequences of their own actions? They have incrementally been separated from the land, from their factories, from creating art, and now they even abandon marriage and reproduction.

"Ah, I see you nodding your heads. Now you understand why, when people first join our church, they are encouraged to jump into group activities. Farming at the rooftop gardens for a week often gives our lay members a greater sense of community than they have ever felt in their entire lives. We also hear wonderful stories of people who never thought they had any musical aptitude—but given the breathing room and a nonjudgmental opportunity to explore, they now share their beautiful singing voices in our choir. Indeed, it is often the little moments of creative expression that provide more joy than the ten thousand songs contained in one's electronic device.

"This is the power that we are giving back to everyday people. Because since the dawn of the internet, our species has been racing madly toward Andy Warhol's fifteen minutes of fame. But along the way, this road somehow became perverted, and now we all dread our own fifteen seconds of shame.

"Mod bless the Prescient One for establishing this church as a proving ground to help us find another way. Because although our religion sprang out of reactionary principles—using modesty as a bulwark against the all-seeing eye—the baton is willingly offered to any member whose insights can help grow the spiritual component.

"Beyond the intangible, we also offer a return to the ways of small-town community life, where everyone is respected and contributes however they can. It is a rebirth of intimacy with materials through craftsmanship, thus restoring purpose to hands whose only function was to swipe across plastic screens. It reinvigorates minds which could critique food but had never prepared a meal of their own.

"People have mocked us for this approach. Saying that we are similar to the Amish, or that we pick and choose which decades we prefer to live in. But is it wrong to want the tools that mankind has developed to serve us? What is there to condemn in wanting to assess which features work and don't work, rather than just blindly accepting everything that has been created? Is it a sin to seek a way of life in which each person is able to fulfill their potential?"

A younger man arose from the crowd. He said, "I think it's fear that causes them to ridicule us. Look how large the church has grown nationwide in the last year alone."

"Tell me, Brother Byron, who is afraid of us?"

"Any number of groups that risk losing market share if we succeed. For one, other religions which have gotten so bogged down by dogma, that they are paralyzed and cannot address this world which is in flux. Governments and corporations and the military all have so much to lose if we keep expanding."

"That is a bold claim. Please, enlighten us."

"People who are happy, self-sufficient, and at peace within a community do not give those entities much to work with. We have weaned thousands of our members off of prescription drugs. And Modestians are not desperate for money, nor so empty that we need to buy trinkets and—"

"Just because we *live* in a shopping mall doesn't mean…"

All the men gave a hearty laugh as the elder trailed off.

"To conclude my idea," the young man said, "the military cannot recruit us because Modestianity has no history of quarrels with other religions. Indeed the enemy today isn't human at all, but the surveillance technology and its tendrils run amok. We are the antidote to that techno-punitive future, that hellscape where it is far more likely that databases will be used to provide evidence of people's crimes and little sins, rather than to compile a highlight reel of their most loving moments or deeds of charity."

"Well said, young man. I commend your insights. But if I may suggest, perhaps you're only half-correct on that final point. Because part of the enemy *does* live within each of us. Only through controlling our hearts and our minds, can we redirect the fiery urges of the flesh and comport ourselves in a dignified manner."

"Amen," several of the men murmured.

"Yes," the elder chuckled, "somehow our map always leads back home. The sacred code of circumspection as the path to the good life, proven correct yet again. And that seems a fitting end note for this wonderful evening.

"Now, it has been a robust six months for the novitiates who advance tomorrow. I bid you to sleep well tonight, because more responsibilities and training await you in your new role as either kinsman or elder. Let us pray…"

"Hail Mody, full of pause," the group recited, "thy patience is with me. Cautious art thou weighing options and cautious is the path of thy life's work. Holy Mody, guide of the future, calm our heartbeats, now and in times of tension. Amen."

The mapmaking session concluded, and as the men were walking back toward the cloisters, they passed a column of female novitiates also returning to their quarters.

"Good evening, sister," the men said quietly.

"Same to you, brother," the women replied.

The sound of shuffling feet filled the silent hallways. At this hour, most other Mall residents had also gone to their lodgings for the night. While there was no formal curfew, by nine o'clock almost all activities had ended and the cuisine courts were closed.

Bill and his comrades entered the cloisters and went into the locker room-style facilities. After brushing their teeth and washing their faces, they retired to the sleeping quarters of bunk beds that had been modified into pods. This was the one taste of privacy novitiates were afforded during their trial period. (All higher ranking members slept in small monk's cells, except in the cases of families, who lived in apartments which had been built into former storefronts.)

Bill climbed into his rectangular sleep pod and zipped the edges shut. He turned on the lamp and fished out his diary from a tiny bookshelf, then eased himself under the covers. He unlocked the book by placing his thumb on a front sensor, then began to write by hand.

"October 25th. Another fulfilling day here at the Mall. Anticipation about tomorrow's festivities is palpable, but we were still able to stay on task and have a productive mapmaking session tonight.

"But how can I forget our performance this afternoon! My dance troupe debuted a new movement to end our sequence. It was just... thrilling! There is something about being here at the Mall that gives my life a sense of richness and fulfillment that nothing from the old days can touch.

"Hitting home runs back in college was a rush, but that was all for the fans. Closing... deals for my bosses also never brought me this kind of personal satisfaction. But now the dancing, the community work, the learning in earnest... Something has awoken in me, and for the first time I feel able to fully express what resides in the depths of my soul.

"This symbiosis of the self resonating with others in truthful purity, that is my ultimate breakthrough. The secrets that I have kept from my brothers will now become the lies that I tell my superiors. For I know that after today's profound revelation, I can never go back to the real world.

"I truly am a Modestian for the first time. I will endure the consequences of letting down those who had entrusted me to perform an important job. Because now I clearly see a flicker of what our leader the Prescient One sees, namely that our society is on a collision course with an existential crisis it is not prepared for.

"It's funny how at first these Modestians can come across as paranoid, eccentric, even borderline agoraphobic. But this religion's evolving vision for how to face the future is the best that I have seen offered by anyone so far. They may not be the richest or most powerful church, but this unlikely gathering speaks from unguarded hearts. I believe that this lack of guile has protected them from falling into any of the traps that usually do 'cults' in.

"I pray that Mod shines upon us in the coming months as the church continues to grow. Just as I hope to be of honorable use to my fellow brothers and sisters. Now I must rest..."

At dawn the cloisters were already bustling and full of chatter. The candidates for advancement bathed quickly and then put on long tunics of shimmering silver that were only worn on special occasions.

They bypassed morning banquet and took escalators up to the third floor, then marched toward the Hall of Emissaries. This is where the inner circle of high ranking church officials lived and worked.

The thirty male candidates entered a waiting area full of plush blue couches accented by silver pillows. An elderly kinsman greeted them with stoic grace.

"Blessed morning to you, gentlemen. Please make yourselves comfortable. You will be called into your interviews shortly, and in no particular order. Refreshments are available on the table beside the far wall—although I, like most others on this momentous day, could barely manage a sip of water until all was known."

The kinsman now acted as usher, escorting the novitiates and pointing to couches they might wish to take. He smiled at Bill and motioned to a nearby cushion.

Bill sat and said, "Thank you, kinsman."

He waited in silence, patiently enduring the butterflies in his stomach while imagining that he too was a caterpillar about to be transformed.

One by one, his brothers were beckoned and taken into a private chamber. He didn't see them come out afterward and assumed they had left by a separate exit —best not to expose their joy or disappointment to those still waiting.

A tap on Bill's shoulder.

"Brother Evans? It is time."

The kinsman smiled graciously and opened a heavy

door, then led him down a hallway with carpet so dense that their feet barely made a sound. Finally they stepped into a small blue room whose lights had been set low. A man of sixty sat in an antique brown chair with velvet upholstery.

"Good morning, novitiate," the man said. "I am Emissary Karlov. Please sit down."

Bill sat in an identical chair facing him and said, "Esteemed Emissary, I am honored to be in your presence today."

"Mod be praised, thank you. Now, my son, I have received positive reports from the elders. They say that you are one of our most well-rounded pupils."

"I have only done what was expected of someone who had chosen this path. If I have stood out from my brothers, I hope it is neither seen as pride on my part, nor a defect on theirs."

"Most certainly not," Karlov said. "One's commitment is the most important aspect. Beyond that, there is room here for all to express their strengths."

"I see," Bill said. "That is good indeed."

"Our only wonder is that you don't appear to have any weaknesses."

"Please, Emissary, you flatter me. I don't know if that assessment is true, or if I even deserve it."

"We shall see," Karlov said. "What concerns me is the perceived gap between your old life and its troubles, compared to the heroic man I see sitting before me today."

"I don't quite understand what you're asking," Bill said. "Please forgive my blindness."

"Brother Evans, I am not trying to embarrass you by making you relive your humiliation. But I must say that having one's wife begin an affair with a neighbor after she discovered that he had been spying on her... It is a devastating blow, and no surprise that you would come running into the arms of Modestianity. But your remarkable turnaround? I scarcely know how it has been possible, and I am as firm a believer as the Prescient One Himself."

"I appreciate your candor. The best answer I can give is that it is not merely the religion itself, or even the teachings, that have affected me so. It has been the full immersion into a community aimed not just at a life lived well, but with conscience. And we see the fruits each day—especially over the past weeks as the influx of refugees has tested our capacities. After all of this, I feel as if I am a whole man and ready for the responsibilities of an elder."

The emissary folded his arms and rested them on his belly.

"I believe in your sincerity," he said. "It's just that a number of people have joined the church due to similar, shall we say, destabilizing moments where technology was somehow involved. We've found that being a lay member offers them the comfort they need, but sadly they're often not fit even for the light duties of a kinsman. Brother Evans, you have done remarkably well as a novitiate. But I must know not only what is *in* your heart, but if you *have* the heart for the life of an elder."

"Blessed Emissary," Bill said, "I understand your concerns and know they come from a place of love. It has been a trying probation period for me indeed. But just yesterday at the theater, while standing for applause with my fellow dancers, I felt a tingle at the base of my head and neck. My mind began floating in a heavenly haze that I have only felt a few other times in my entire life. And for me it is the most wonderful feeling of all—like I am not alone, I can set down my burden, and need not pretend or hide from anyone. After that feeling of lightness fades, however, I want to weep because I don't know how many years of numbness or pain will pass before some other unexpected moment returns me to that mist.

"It was no fluke that it happened to me here at the Mall," Evans continued, "where I live among people of all backgrounds, and whose common bond is that they choose to take life seriously. If I had previously felt weak or on the verge of faltering, no such threat to my resolve exists now. I am ready to advance so that I may serve."

The emissary closed his eyes and exhaled audibly through his nose. "Your heart within hearts has spoken," he said. "I cannot stand in the way of a man who shows such determination in the face of life's trials. I congratulate you, Brother Evans, for soon you shall be an elder! Go prepare for the ceremony."

Bill stood up and grabbed hold of Karlov's hand, then placed the crown of his own head in its grasp.

"Thank you, Emissary. This is the greatest day of my life."

Bill was escorted to the exit by a different kinsman, then breezed down one of the large open foyers as if in a trance. He made his way down to the amphitheater where the advancement ceremony would shortly begin, then sat down among his brothers feeling utter contentment. They spoke of this and of that, but Bill barely heard what was said, so great was the joy pulsing in his soul.

When the ceremony began, he gazed upon the many church members in the audience through misty eyes. He saw the royal procession walk across the stage, heard the lofty pronouncements, and finally the Prescient One appeared to great fanfare.

After several brief scripture readings, the new kinsmen and kinswomen were announced. These twenty crossed the stage, each shaking hands with a proponent as well as receiving a nod from the Prescient One, who was seated among the church leaders nearby.

Next, Bill and the other novitiates being promoted to elder went up to the stage. As each name was called, one member of the group crossed over and embraced both an emissary and a proponent. The Prescient One, who had risen and come forward, also offered a quiet word of blessing.

Bill heard his name called and stepped out into the open. He smiled as the audience applauded, then felt real tears well up as first the emissary, and then the proponent, took him into their arms.

He nearly broke down when he heard the name "Elder Evans" announced over the loudspeaker as he approached the Prescient One. The figurehead was absolutely glistening in his silver robe, and his blue-painted face was as smooth as cast acrylic.

Bill searched for the right words to express his joy and gratitude, but felt his veins turn to ice when the Prescient One leaned in and said, "Congratulations, Marcus." He tried to pull back as a wave of nausea constricted his stomach, but the other man held him firm and whispered, "It's alright. You have nothing to fear. I know exactly where your mind is. For now, focus on your new role as elder. But soon we will meet privately. Because you and I have great work to do together!"

He left the stage in complete shock. Rather than join the other freshly anointed elders in celebration, he wandered out of the amphitheater and found a secluded corner to sit in. He dropped his head into his hands as the same thought echoed in his mind over and over.

How can he possibly know that I work for the FBI?

8. THE WAR ROOM

Eleven days out from the election, the president and a dozen of her staff gathered around the Roosevelt Room's long table for a ten o'clock briefing.

"Okay, people," Eileen Jeffries-Lao said, "let's lay it all out. Give me whatever you've got, good or bad. Then we can head into the weekend knowing where we stand and what we need to do for the final push. Bottom line, we've got to get this HRA business shored up right now, or the next ten years will be a disaster. If Dominguez wins—even if he doesn't actually dismantle the administration—he'll find a way to run it into the ground.

"Millions of Beneficiaries will suffer as a result. Grandmothers trying to pay for their groceries will find a zero balance on their debit cards. And overseas—my God—what country would actually follow our lead and go through with their own version of Reparations if we fail? I cannot stress enough the magnitude of what's at stake. Now, Tony, let's start with you."

Chief of Staff Tony Rizzuto stepped forward and

handed binders to all the staffers.

"Thank you, Madam President," he said. "The whole team is here to deliver for you. The first order of business is keeping the peace. The bad press we get from every vandalized field office could cost us a hundred votes. We're already working with the National Guard and local law enforcement in high-sensitivity areas. Plus we've provided them with additional access to the surveillance grid, as well as our S'more Stopper teams. At every large gathering, our smart camera network will relay the data and deploy any necessary countermeasures.

"Next up," Tony continued, "news on our opponent. Victor Dominguez will be sweeping across the southern states this weekend. Natalie, can you fill us in on the details?"

A female staffer seated at the table consulted her tablet, then a series of graphics and charts appeared on the projector screen.

"Look at what he's doing," Natalie said. "Heading straight into the heart of Reparations country to stir things up. Louisiana, Mississippi, Alabama, Georgia, and Florida. He's calling his speech 'A Better Way Forward.' From the intel we've gathered at other recent events, Dominguez has been testing the waters by slowly ramping up his anti-HRA rhetoric."

The president clucked her tongue. "So he's going for broke right now. Into the belly of the beast! I admire his guts, even if he's out of his league. What I want to know is how much of what he's doing is deliberately planned, versus his campaign just winging it?"

"Madam President, if I may continue?" Natalie said.

"You know what? Everybody just call me by my first name for now. We're getting our hands dirty here.

If we patch this dam before it bursts out onto the country, then by all means, I'll be proud to still be addressed by my formal title after Election Day."

"Sure thing, Eileen. Here are clips from two recent Dominguez speeches given a week apart. First, here he is in Houston last Saturday."

The image of Victor Dominguez appeared on screen. He said, "This Reparations thing is like a road trip that wasn't fully planned. Sure, you stocked the car full of food and supplies, but you didn't consult the map and now you're stuck in a ditch. So you have to call Victor's Towing Service to pull your car out, make any necessary repairs, and get back on the road."

"Next," Natalie said, "the speech yesterday in Philadelphia."

"When you get old or sick," Dominguez said, crossing a stage where dozens of people in matching red t-shirts stood behind him, "you can't always do what you want to do. So you go to the doctor and he explains what's going on. I, Dr. Dominguez, and my expert staff have done all the tests. We've looked at the charts, and honestly the prognosis for this Reparations program does not look good. Mr. and Mrs. Beneficiary, I'm very sorry. We may be able to repair the broken bones, but after this kind of a fall, I don't think the program will ever walk again."

"No!" The president slapped her thigh. "Tell me he didn't go there. Can you believe these metaphors he's using? Is he actually calling himself the Mexican mechanic? Sure, vote *him* in! My god, who's writing these speeches?"

"I know, it's ridiculous," Tony said. "And normally it would be a laughing matter, if he didn't keep gaining in the polls. Kwame, can you give us the latest on that?"

"Of course." A thin Afrigro-American with shiny shaved head stood up. "After the debate last week—Dominguez's coming out party, according to the media—he got a sizable bump which then settled back down. So here's the full array: two weeks ago, we were up sixty-two to thirty-four. By last Friday, the margin had shrunk to fifty-eight to thirty-nine. And as of today, it stands at fifty-four to forty-four. The remaining percentage points are distributed among the two independent candidates."

"So he's slowly cutting in, bite by bite," Eileen said. "Interesting that he's now choosing to take on the South so aggressively. You'd think if he was looking for a few points, he'd head into the Rust Belt and play his violin for all the disgruntled Caucs out there."

"My information suggests that Dominguez's people are as much on a fact-finding mission as they are trying to gain votes. So the reception he gets from the diverse southern crowd will probably determine where he travels next week."

"I'll be damned. They *are* making it up as they go. They don't even know which states they might be able to snipe from us. But something's working. So how does all that impact where we're going?"

Tony spoke up. "We're still on schedule to hit the cities we booked when this was all just a victory tour. That said, we'll add some small town stops to meet with the locals in between the bigger speeches."

"Also," Natalie added, "we've got you scheduled to record several promo spots when you're in New York on Monday. Mostly national stuff, maybe one or two tailored to a state race. Plus, we came up with the idea of putting you alongside a guest which might help restore confidence in the HRA."

"And who might that be?" Eileen said.

"Kate Donohugh."

"What?! The one from that *DDM TV* disaster? Are you crazy?"

"Look," Tony said. "She's composed, photogenic, even has the cancer survivor angle. Did you see when they put her face to face with that fugitive DDM in the hospital? It was *compelling*. Truth is, Kate's a part of the zeitgeist now, and we can make her into whatever we want. She was also one of the HRA's earliest advocates long before she ended up working there, so you're not likely to find a bigger supporter of the program."

"And now," the president said, "it's all unraveling in front of her eyes. People like her care more about Reparations than you, me, and even a hell of a lot of blacks. Damn, damn, damn. You all might be onto something. Use these ads to recharge the base of true believers that started this whole thing."

"Exactly. Remind them that they're just like the Abolitionists of the nineteenth century. Up against the odds, but on the right side of history. So they can't quit. It's too important of a mission to let a few stumbles derail the whole thing."

"It's time to rally the troops again. Rebuild their faith in the HRA. Because I will *not* preside over another failure like Obamacare! Do you all hear me?"

"Yes, of course. But please," Tony said, lowering his hands slowly, "try to stay calm. We're all here as a team. A winning team. We'll make the right plan and focus like a laser."

"Okay, I'm taking a breath. But tell me, what have you got on the Sentinels?"

"After the private message they sent following the first hack, one of their members has been communicating with us behind the scenes ever since."

"Unreal. What's the newest intel?"

"Their liaison insists that they'll continue to stand down and will not foment any unrest, as long as we work with them in acquiescing to their demands regarding the HRA. Not that we will, but…"

"Never mind that. Just keep them talking. They may be men of their word for now, but I still intend to capture them, shut them down, and if the polls support it, bring them to justice. For now though, we do need to show the public something encouraging on this front. I can't believe that none of our agencies—who are always tooting their own horns, I might add—they still haven't caught anyone yet. How is that even possible with all the people they've interviewed?"

"I assure you, there are numerous persons of interest being moved up the list for tighter scrutiny."

"Oh hell, we're *all* under scrutiny now! You've got to give me more than that."

"What I'm trying to say, Eileen, is that we don't want to tip off the big players by taking any low-level moles into custody."

"Tony, that may sound sensible, but right now I need some damn arrests! And on camera too. Good optics to help secure the vote of every last person who's on the fence about whether I'm cut out for the job after all. You know… We're just gonna have to fake it. Hire a couple actors and put on a good show. I'm sorry, but this is where we are."

"Very well," Tony said after a pause. "If that's what you want. Is there any particular… racial and gender configuration that you'd prefer?"

"Same as pretty much every other hacker. Cauc. Male. And… balding! Drag a guy with a comb-over in front of the cameras."

"Consider it done. How about we give him a lazy

eye while we're at it?"

"That's the spirit! Aw, don't look so glum, everyone. In eleven days we'll be popping champagne and getting drunk as hell! And then we can get back to work for real. I promise you."

"All in good time, Eileen. First, let's win this thing."

The president stood up and leaned forward with her hands on the table.

"Damn," she muttered. "A month ago we were sitting pretty. Oblivious. In dreamland, coasting toward re-election."

"And then just like that—" Tony snapped his fingers.

"Just like that, we're about to serve up the White House to the next Jimmy Carter."

"I need a drink. Victor Dominguez will *not* become president on our watch. He has a pet iguana named Tito, for Christ's sake."

"And his wife is always out running marathons in those skimpy neon shorts. That freckled fool is thin as a rail!"

"Okay, I think the idea of there being a *first lady* next year is all the motivation this group needs to get back on track."

"Speaking of which," Eileen said, "does anybody know the whereabouts of my husband?"

Everyone looked at each other sheepishly.

"No one? I don't care what he's up to, believe me. I am completely focused on this campaign. Knowing where he can be found is just one part of my master checklist."

"I believe," one young staffer mustered, "that the *Beltway Times* posted a picture of Mr. Jeffries with one of the, um, female golf pros over at Congressional."

"Okay, fine. So he's in the area. Moving on!"

Tony consulted his binder. "We've heard rumblings that some advocacy groups are nervous. They're not happy about Dominguez rising in the polls every time he opens his mouth and says something more derogatory about the HRA."

"Assure them that all this Dominguez talk is just hype and scare tactics. He's been riding a lucky wave that's about to crash badly. We're solid as a rock and will put him away soon enough."

"The NAACP still has full confidence in you. They say they're happy to send out an email blast in support, if we can provide them with a quote."

"Of course. Someone record this. 'I was proud to stand beside the NAACP as we fought to secure long-overdue Reparations for the oppressed people of this country. I am honored to know that this prestigious organization still supports me as we resist those who would seek to defeat us before our noble task is complete.' "

"Got it. Moving on. The stock market has mostly bounced back from its initial post-hack lows, though trading volumes are lower than normal."

"We're in the hold-your-breath phase. Probably will be like that all next week, unless the polls show good separation back in our favor."

"Exactly. Next up, overseas there were a couple of bombings by the usual suspects. Ten dead in Egypt, thirty-five over in Iraq. Anything you want to include in our statement?"

"Go with boilerplate as long as no American citizens died. We've got too much going on to deal with that right now."

"Right. Finally, at least for my list, are battleground state updates in other elections. Looks like we'll take the governors races in Florida and Oregon—"

"We'd better! How on earth did we lose Oregon back in 'twenty-two? It feels like we're in a battleground *nation* right now. Please, go on."

"And in the Senate, it could be a wash. Up in North Carolina and Pennsylvania, but down in Colorado, and if you can believe it, California."

"If things were on firmer ground here, I'd be happy to fly out and give a speech or two. But as it all stands right now, I'm sorry to say that they might be on their own."

"I'll relay a message saying that 'the president sincerely regrets that prior commitments preclude her from offering in-person support.' "

"You're a hell of a translator, Tony. Okay, let's wrap this up. Is there any *good* news to report?"

Natalie raised her hand. "One thing that seems to have gotten lost in the shuffle is the grand opening out in Las Vegas this weekend."

"Oh, that's right!" The president rubbed her hands together. "Wow. I know we didn't plan it this way, but the timing could be perfect. Please tell me they're promoting the hell out of it."

"I believe," Tony said, "there's going to be a TV special hosted by none other than Ryan Richards."

"What, is everyone from *DDM* looking for redemption now? Regardless, clear my schedule for that time slot. And you're all invited. We'll get some snacks, vodka, beer. Let's have a little pre-party before the final push. It's Vegas, guys. Come on!"

"And we're going to win."

"God damn right we are."

9. PAYBACK

"Now, coming to you from Las Vegas, Nevada… Please welcome the host of *DDM TV Live*, the one and only, Ryan Richards!"

Applause roared through a crowded casino as spotlights darted around wildly. Big band music brought out a dancing Ryan Richards, whose face was so bronze it was as if he had stepped directly out of a tanning booth and onto the stage. He smiled and waved to the audience as he strutted forward, then raised a pencil-thin silver microphone to his lips.

"What a difference a few weeks can make, eh folks?" he said with a wry grin. The crowd gave hearty laughter. "But how fitting that one of the world's premier boxing cities is where we scrape ourselves off the mat, and come out swinging with a combo of our own. Ladies and gentlemen, are you ready to gamblllllle!"

Everyone yelled and waved their arms. Hip-hop began to play as camera-mounted drones circled above the casino floor, revealing a sea of slot machines and video poker units, plus dozens of gaming tables. As the cheers died down, Richards pulled a wad of cash from his pocket and motioned as if to hand a bill to a member of the audience, before yanking it away playfully.

"Got ya! Oh, I see we have some spooky Halloween costumes out there in the crowd. Hopefully you'll bag some treats tonight. Now, why are we all the way out west, and not back in our New York studios? Because we're celebrating this very special new casino which offers a unique twist on gambling. Ladies and gentlemen, it's Paybax time!"

As the crowd erupted once more, giant video screens near the stage showed endless streams of gold coins pouring down into a pair of brown hands. Richards began peeling off bills from his stack and throwing them into the crowd, then stepped back with a wave.

"Sorry, sorry. That wasn't supposed to be part of the show. I just couldn't contain my excitement. We're having too much of a good time tonight! So, what is this place all about? Consider the name: Paybax. Who is doing the paying, and who is getting paid back? Hmm…"

Richards pointed to a paunchy white woman in her fifties and declared, "You *and* you! 'But Ryan, how can that be?' you ask. Simple. Because all the games here at Paybax Casino are linked with the HRA's accounting framework.

"For every dollar you gamble, one half of one percent is immediately applied to your Debit Score balance. And that's only if you lose! Because if you win, some of that prize money can be used to pay off what you owe—or will owe down the road after MARVIN digs up more dirt, haha.

"Look, we know that Reparations hasn't been much fun for most Debtors. But now, you can reduce your obligation all while getting in on the excitement. That is, if you have the guts to play!"

Loud brass music blared and a series of logos and graphics flashed across the screens. The announcer read, "Come try your luck on one of the many games exclusive only to Paybax Casino. First, take a puff on the Prosperity Pipe. One big win and you'll be spouting Jackpot Theories. Are you brave enough to enter the Haunted Plantation?"

Richards cocked an eyebrow and pursed his lips, then looked dramatically from side to side.

"So far, we've only been talking about Debtors. And this casino isn't some Caucs-only club, now is it? Noooo, zir! Hahaha! There's plenty of fun and games to be had by Beneficiaries as well. Tell 'em, Donnie."

The announcer said, "How about up to two hundred dollars in chips for free? Offer only valid once per Beneficiary per week—sorry, they make us say that. What about one free double-down bet per night? Or, how about a little something we call Spontaneous Reparations? Yes, if you suspect that a Debtor at your table has a better hand than you... Whoosh! You can swap cards. Just yell out 'Houdini!' and the deed will be done—handled by the dealer of course, because there *are* cameras everywhere."

During this interlude, Richards had left the stage and gone out onto the bustling casino floor. He approached an elderly white couple playing Acre's Bounty and said, "Howdy, folks! What brought you to Paybax Casino on opening weekend?"

"Hi, Ryan!" the woman said loudly, trying to be heard over the buzz of the crowd. "We love the nickel slots, so we said why not give this new place a shot?"

"Indeed! How have you fared so far?"

"I'm up a few dollars, but my husband hasn't—oh my goodness! Look, honey! You just got three mules in a row!"

Richards turned to the camera and said, "It can happen to you too, just like that! Come on, let's go meet more people. Aha, it looks like there's high drama over at this Texas free 'em table. Let's watch the action."

Three players looked on intently as the dealer turned the river card. They each placed their final bets, then as the hands were revealed, the black man playing threw his arms up in triumph. The dealer pushed several stacks of chips toward him.

"Looks like we have a winner," Richards beamed, "in more ways than one. Let's mosey on over to the craps table, where it looks like someone's on a bit of a roll."

A young brunette at the head of the table was shaking her fist high in the air. She threw the dice down the length of the table, bouncing them hard against the walls, and watched them settle. The group of people watching roared. She looked at the man standing next to her and he said, "One more time, baby!"

The woman joined her hands as if to pray, then cast the dice forward with her eyes closed. A great cheer arose and she fell into the man's arms crying.

Richards approached them and said, "My, oh my, another big winner! What's your name?"

The woman wiped her eyes. "I'm Stephanie and this is my fiance, Trent. Go Badgers!"

"Oh wow, all the way from Wisconsin. What brought you two kids to Vegas?"

"We each have pretty bad Debit Scores as it is. But when we got the estimate from the MARVIN Marriage Calculator, we almost died when we realized how much our future children would owe."

"Too many DEs?"

"No, no," Trent said. "Turns out we're both distantly related to General Custer."

"Forbidden love, ooh la la!"

"So," Stephanie continued, "we came here to see if Lady Luck would tap us with her magic wand. And now she has! We just won enough money to help reduce our own Debit Scores, plus start a Reparations Fund for our kids."

Richards gave Trent a high-five, then started walking back toward the stage.

"Just amazing," he said. "Paybax truly has all the glitz and excitement of the casinos you know and love. But with the added bonus of poker and slot games that you'll find nowhere else. Now, I know that you folks in the audience can hardly restrain yourselves from joining in the fun, but we've got one more surprise in store, so hold on. A very special guest is here to help me officially get this party started.

"I'd like you to welcome my well-traveled friend—a man who has journeyed from Mexico to California to New York City. A man who took a *little detour* into South Dakota on his way back to Los Angeles, and is now here in Las Vegas for the very first time. Put your hands together for my hero, Mr. Luis Ortega!"

Luis jogged out onto the stage wearing a baseball cap with flipped-up brim and his trademark black-framed glasses. Richards gave him a high-five and Luis waved at the audience.

"My, oh my," Richards crowed. "A reunion that could make the angels sing. How are ya, old man?"

"I'm good," Luis said. "Feeling well rested."

People in the crowd said, "Awwww," and put their hands on their hearts.

Richards escorted Luis across the stage to a giant faux-stone disc that towered above them. Similar to Italy's Mouth of Truth and the Aztec calendar stone, it had ornate nooks and crannies, cryptic inscriptions, downcast hollow eyes, and a gaping lower jaw that protruded like a toll booth collection basket.

"Oh boy, Luis. This is it, the main attraction here at Paybax Casino. Because every hour on the hour, they'll hold a ceremony here at MARVIN'S Mouth so that people can pay tribute to Reparations. And joining us to demonstrate how it works is Frank, a Debtor who won five thousand dollars playing Repatriated Artifacts earlier today. Frank, come on up and tell us how much you would like to keep, apply to your debt, plus do our variation on 'phone a friend.' "

"Hi, world! Frank Turgeson here. How about I keep half, apply forty percent to my Score, and pay the rest of my chips *forward* to Luis?"

"Wha-what?!" Richards screeched as he fell to his knees. "Payin' it back! Payin' it forward! Sing it with me, folks. We're payin' it back, by payin' it forward..."

Richards began a ridiculous dance as he repeated this refrain. A bass drum began to thump from somewhere. Fred threw his hands out to raise the roof. Luis looked offstage, nodded at someone, then started to dance as well. Richards caught his breath and motioned for them to stop.

"Now," Richards said, "let's see the process in action. Frank, step up to the left side like so, just let the stone take a quick retinal scan... And now follow the instructions on the touchscreen to make your selections."

"Feed me!" a deep, craggy voice bellowed from inside the monolith. "Feed me!"

Frank dumped his chips and tokens into the wide

open mouth. The sound of crunching and cash register dings filled the casino. Richards motioned for Luis to come closer.

"Luis, now you just need to scan your eye and—"

A siren wailed and a torrent of silver coins shot out of the eyes onto the ground below.

"Go on, buddy. Take them all. That's yours to gamble now."

Luis knelt down and put some of the money into his pocket. Richards gave Frank a big hug and said, "Wonderful, just wonderful."

Luis stood up with bulging pockets and Richards asked, "Is there anything you'd like to say now?"

"Uh, wow. Thank you, Frank. I hope I can win some more out there."

"Anything *else* you'd like to add?"

"Oh yeah, sure." Luis dug a small sheet of paper out from under the coins, then began to read. "In addition to this new casino," he said slowly, "I am here to announce the HRA's new Beneficiary Deferment Program. Of which I am the first participant. That's right, now any Beneficiary who is in school or who has another pressing commitment, can choose to defer their DDM assignment until he or she completes said program. In conclusion, I would like to thank the Historical Reparations Administration for helping me fulfill my dream to become an electrical engineer and make my family proud. The new deferment program— helping the HRA help Beneficiaries like me."

"Well said, young man," Richards added after the crowd gave respectful applause. "Do you hear that, world? 'I prefer to defer!' Because this whole Reparations thing *is* for the Beneficiaries, right? It just took a little healthy civil disobedience to persuade the HRA to accommodate this reasonable request.

Speaking of accommodations, I hear the hotel rooms here are 'suite'!

"Well, that about wraps it up for this special broadcast. For those of you watching at home, be sure to make a stop at Paybax Casino a part of your next Vegas vacation. Because hey, just one bet could reduce your debt! And to everyone here in person tonight, you've been so patient, but it's finally time to get out there and play. This is Ryan Richards saying good night, and I'll see you out on the casino floor!"

The crowd hollered one last time before flowing out into the gaming area, and lively brass music piped through the speakers to end the show. Richards skipped off the stage and grabbed a napkin to mop his forehead. He took in the lively scene of tourists having fun amid all the flashing lights and electronic beeps, then gave a big sigh.

He felt a squeeze on the arm and saw that it was Gayle, his *DDM* producer who had flown out to oversee the broadcast.

"Ry Guy!" she beamed. "That was great. You really went the extra mile for us out there."

Richards wiped more sweat off his temple. "Aw, shucks. And likewise. The whole crew was on point. Excellent show. And hey, no hacks or protesters out on the casino floor, so I guess security actually did their job."

"Yep, everyone pitched in. But seriously, Ryan. You delivered! Huge energy and stage presence. That was a command performance and you should be proud."

"It's all about embracing the moment, Gayle. Sometimes you've just got to be on."

"I hope the people in high places who were watching appreciated it."

"Well, if darling Eileen wins, maybe she'll invite me to emcee an event sometime. Because if she loses—"

"No one's going to lose."

"*If she loses,* I may never work again."

"I swear, sometimes you take hyperbole to the extreme."

"Okay, fine. Relegated to a cooking show or selling magic glue on an infomercial. Heh, worst case, I'll get stuck hosting a game show on Lifetime."

"Are you kidding? That would be your dream job, getting housewives all hot and bothered. Anyway, we've done our part. Why don't you go take a load off?"

"That's easy for you to say. You live behind the camera. I'm all amped up right now. Buuuut, I see someone who might relate. Luis! What's up, buddy?"

Richards ran over to Luis and gave him a high-five.

"Hi there, Mister Ryan."

"Great job out there, man. It all went off like a charm."

"Cool. So nobody took over the show this time? I'm glad."

"You and me both, buddy." Richards turned his eyes into slits and scanned the surrounding area. "But now it's time to see what kind of trouble I can get into. You up for a quick drink over at the bar?"

"Nah. I'll go find my parents, see what they wanna do."

"Aw, come on. Luis! It's me! I sat by your bedside, remember? Let's go shoot the shit until your folks turn up."

"Okay, I guess. Let me just text them real quick."

An hour later, Ryan Richards was twirling a cocktail umbrella between his fingers and saying, "Here's the thing, bud. You gotta learn to loosen up.

Like earlier, when you were worried they wouldn't serve you because you're under twenty-one."

"I know, I'm sorry."

"Because Luis, it's Vegas! Brand new casino and everything. And hell, it's almost like a private party with all the crew members and HRA people around. Plus, who's gonna say no to me? I'm Ryan Effing Richards. Having a night out with my main man, Luis *El Boracho* Ortega!"

Luis cracked a smile and gulped some beer. "Nah, I'm not as cool as you. Tall *gringo* with the really white teeth, haha."

"Ah, come off that humble crap," Richards grumbled as he poked at the ice in his glass. "It's smooth, though. Like you've got your own vibe. Sitting back in the pocket. Doing things on Ortega time."

"Hmm. What time is that, exactly?"

"Time for some shots, that's what! Hey, girly! Two shots of Patrón Silver, *por favor*."

Luis looked down at his phone while the bartender came over and poured their drinks.

"Oh man, where are my parents anyway?"

"Probably out gambling or watching some circus show bullshit. I tell you what. Let's stop worrying about them and take on the town! I'm a real celebrity. I still got some street cred from my old acting days. Annnnd, I could probably get us in VIP at some strip clubs!"

"Nah… You mean, like, naked girls?"

"Hotties. Nude. Full bar. And maybe even some *private dances!*"

"Dang. Can you like, touch 'em?"

"Well, you're not really supposed to—but it don't matter if you're VIP!"

"Crap, why won't my parents pick up?"

"Forget 'em, man. We're in Vegas, on the Strip! Are you in, or am I gonna have to handle all the girls myself?"

"No way! You probably get lots of chicks because you're famous, but—" Luis downed his shot of tequila "—now I've been on TV too, like twice. That's gotta be worth something. So let's go, *cabrón!*"

Ryan drank his shot and gave a howl. "Luis, about to get dowwwwn!"

The next morning, Luis woke up to a steady banging sound. His body ached from head to toe, so he just stayed curled up. But the noise didn't stop. Finally he dragged himself out of bed to see what it was. The banging was coming from the door that connected with his parents' suite.

He called out, "Who's there? What do you want?"

"Luis!" his mom cried. "Are you okay?"

"Of course, I'm fine. What's the problem, Mama?"

"Please, can you open the door?"

Luis unlocked the door and then ran to put on a bathrobe. His mother and father came into the room and embraced him.

"Thank the Lord!" his mother said. "We didn't know what happened to you."

Luis eased out of their arms and fell into a chair. "But last night I couldn't find you after the show. Where did you go?"

Mr. Ortega said, "Seeing you on the stage made us too nervous, so we walked down the street. We looked inside the casinos. They were all very nice."

"Plus we did some gambling!" Mrs Ortega said. "But only just a little. Papi won fifty dollars one time. Then we got a little lost, and when your father checked his phone for the map, he sees that the battery is dead. I don't have my phone, so what do we do?"

"Finally we get back to this casino and ask for you, but somebody say you leave here in a fancy car. I plug my phone and try to call you, but I get your voicemail."

"Sorry," Luis said. "I guess I turned my phone off."

"It's okay. We were tired. We think you must be having fun with the people from the television. But now this morning you don't wake up, you don't answer the phone… Your mama gets worried so she knocks on the door."

"But now we see everything is fine," Mrs. Ortega said. "Did you have a good time?"

Luis scratched his head. "I think so."

"Okay, you go take a shower. Then we get breakfast and leave for the airport."

"Sure, Mama. See you soon."

Luis got back into bed and tried to remember what had happened the previous night. Vague memories of vodka bottles and dancing to techno flickered in his mind. Then he noticed that the sugary smell of female fragrance was still on his own body. He found his glasses under the bedside table and put them on. One lens was covered with a neon green imprint of kissing lips.

Now very intrigued, Luis crawled over to his jeans which were on the floor and took his phone out of the pocket. He turned it on to discover that not only was Ryan Richards now one of his contacts, the man had in fact sent him over a dozen photo messages.

The final picture showed Luis hugging a topless woman, while Richards was bent over pretending to bite his backside. The accompanying text message said, "Don't tell MARVIN!"

Luis wrote back, "omg. i dont remember half that stuff".

"Doesn't matter," Richards replied a few minutes later. "I'm sure I'll be out in LA soon. We'll do Hollywood together in style…"

"Haha ur crazy. Oh and thank u. I had fun!"

"And you sir are a legend. Rock on!"

Luis nestled under the covers and slowly scrolled through the pictures again, blushing as he relived his wild night in Sin City.

10. FACE TO FACE

When Kate arrived at the Newark HRA megabranch early Monday morning, she was relieved to find that all the protesters she'd seen the previous week were gone. The Debtor and Beneficiary lines were also considerably shorter than before, so even though several National Guard troops were still posted out front, she hoped this was a sign that public perception was starting to turn in the HRA's favor.

Just over a week ago, while still reeling from the shock of her experience in Virginia, Kate found that it wasn't so easy to turn her back on nearly fifteen years of living when groping for a new way forward. Almost drowsily, she took the path of least resistance and returned home to Brooklyn ready to give everything another shot.

At work she joined in on the nationwide effort to reaffirm that the HRA was functioning reliably. But all the while, she kept her discoveries a secret from everyone—not only her coworkers, but even her husband—because she simply couldn't afford to make any rash decisions without knowing the consequences.

And today she was thanking God for having done it this way. In just a few hours she was expected back in the city to appear in election ads with none other than the President of the United States.

She, Jan, and TJ had sent frantic and excited group texts to each other about it all weekend, and now Kate was not surprised to find them waiting on the couch in her office with big smiles.

"Hi, guys!" she said.

"The ride continues!" Jan said. "Are you ready, girl?"

"I can't believe that this, of all things, is happening."

"You've made it through the lows. Now it's time for a high."

"I'm starting to feel nervous. Whew!"

"TJ, tell her the good news so she can calm down."

TJ swiped into a tablet and said, "Dominguez bombed over the weekend. This article here says half the crowd walked out on him both in Mobile and New Orleans."

"Goodness," Kate said. "What went wrong?"

"His mouth, apparently. Listen to this quote. 'Y'all down here been livin' amongst each other for hundreds of years. I reckon you could do a better job handling your business than some far-away government body.' Then someone in the crowd yelled out, 'Are you talking about states' rights?' "

Jan smacked her forehead.

"Well, how did he respond?" Kate said.

TJ chuckled. "That question was a setup. There's no right answer. He gave a hesitant 'yes,' but a 'no' would have pissed people off just as much."

"And," Jan said, "I saw on the news this morning that Jeffries-Lao got a healthy bump in the polls. So

Kate, there's no need to be anxious when you see her."

Kate smiled. "That is good news. I've always wanted to meet her. And I was just dreading the thought that if I did poorly today and she lost, that some part of that would reflect on me."

"Instead you're just going to knock in an insurance run for the team. So have fun! Next week we put all the doubts to rest, and then we'll get back to it in here."

"Full steam ahead."

"I'm counting on you. Just because you got off the hook not going to Cleveland thanks to Luis, don't think we aren't going to work you here!"

"That's right," TJ added. "And now that those FBI snoops have finally moved on, we'll be able to pep everyone up again. Team leaders, unite!"

They came together and gave a group high-five.

At noon, Kate arrived at the studio space in uptown. She passed through a security checkpoint before being escorted to an upper floor. She sat briefly for hair and makeup, where she was also quizzed by a producer as to whether she had reviewed the scripts the president's team had sent over.

Kate was then led to a small holding room, where she found herself face to face and alone with Eileen Jeffries-Lao. She couldn't breathe.

The president smiled broadly and extended her hand. "Hello, Kate. Thank you so much for agreeing to help my campaign on such short notice."

"It's an honor, Madam President. Unexpected, to say the least, but I am at your service."

"Excellent. I wish I could say that I commanded a prepared production crew, but apparently they're still setting up in there. Shall we have coffee while we wait?"

"I'd love to," Kate said.

They sat down at a small wooden dining table. Kate didn't dare break the silence. The president smiled again, then said, "So you live in the city?"

"Yes," Kate said. "My husband and I have an apartment in Brooklyn."

"Kids?"

"No. Two dogs."

"Ah. And from what I gather, you've been with the HRA since the beginning?"

"Even before that, actually. I joined the Colonial Amends Committee in the spring of 'twenty-three."

"Oh," the president said. "I'm a bit surprised we've never met then. The CAC was one of several groups my campaign allied with during that magical journey."

Kate blushed. "I've seen you speak several times. But the occasion never actually brought us together."

"Well, if this roller coaster ride the HRA's been on is what it took to finally introduce us, I hope we'll both be better for it. And truly, I'm appalled that you've been personally impacted during this trying time."

"That's so kind of you to say, Madam President."

"Please, it's Eileen for everyone between now and the victory party."

"Okay," Kate said, "I'll do my best to remember that."

The president flipped through some papers, making small notes in the margins. She looked up at Kate. "So, you're an assistant regional manager. How high up do you want to go with the HRA?"

Kate set down her coffee and brought an index finger to her lips for a moment. "I can't say for certain. I've always just wanted to help people. That's been my motivation. So even though today, while I have an impressive-sounding job title and more management responsibilities than if I was working at a women's shelter, the core sentiment remains the same."

"Interesting." Eileen paused, then said, "I do think that people with real talent shouldn't let the idea of 'service' get in the way of making the right decisions for themselves. Our movement can't afford it, in fact."

"How so?" Kate asked.

"Because stunting your own potential, by being passive rather than planning, only hurts those in need. There will always be someone out there going through hard times. Do you have the energy for that kind of a life? Down in the trenches, always fighting, fighting, fighting for the underdog?"

"I have, so far. And that's what led me to being part of the surge that made the HRA possible."

"Kate, when you're in your twenties, it's all fresh and exciting. And with the HRA you rode a timely wave into, if we're going to be honest, the rock star world. Big new agency, fancy new building, a nice income for yourself. But now that there's been a hiccup…"

"What am I supposed to say?"

"The point is," Jeffries-Lao said, "even after we clamp down on the Sentinels, take some time to think about where your life is headed. If you stay where you are while the program runs its course, it might become less fulfilling each year. Or maybe you could use your experience to help when we launch overseas."

Kate said, "I'm not sure what that would mean for my marriage."

"Exactly. These are the types of considerations we have to make as we get older. There's other fields, other options."

"But I don't know if anything will be as rewarding as what I'm doing now."

"Oh, I believe you," Eileen said. "But it was the rarest of opportunities that sprang up only because all the right conditions arose. So maybe before you move onto something new, take stock and see what it is you really want in life."

"Forgive me," Kate said, "if I'm a bit shocked to hear you put it so bluntly. It seems as if all you've ever done is serve."

The president sat back in her chair. "If you look at my resume more closely," she said, "you'll notice several small gaps between the major moves. Each time I considered taking that leap—from local to state to national politics—I briefly stepped away. First, to live a little, but also to consult with my family. Because they're in it just as much as you. Have you talked with your husband about what might happen if I were to lose next week?"

Kate looked away for a moment. "The truth is that since being sent to South Dakota to deal with the Luis Ortega situation, I haven't been communicating with Chris very well. And when I was away, I even made some upsetting discoveries about my education that have knocked my equilibrium out of whack.

"But," she continued, "I've put too many years into my work, and the HRA needs all the support it can get right now—so I stuffed the doubt back down and just soldiered on. And here we are. I'm unsure whether what you're saying is supposed to snap me back in line, or if it will end up leaving me even more confused."

"That's just what we call the life of a career woman," Eileen said with a smile. "They pump us up as little girls, assuring us that we can 'have it all.' As if feminism and advantageous hiring practices magically make it so that we don't have to sacrifice or give our all.

"You can't legislate respect. You can't control where men's eyes wander. And when you have children, even an accommodating country like ours can't carry the baby for you. It can't clear your mind to focus on work when you're swooning with nausea. So you see, even when things are at their best, nothing's perfect. And that's why, yes, some of this does have to be only about you."

Kate smiled. "I'll take this advice to heart, thank you. But after you win, how could I in good conscience step away anytime soon?"

"How old are you now?" the president asked.

"Thirty-two."

"Here's a little tidbit, just between us warrior princesses. From nine to five, keep working as you have been. But when you get home at night, really be present with your husband. And who knows, maybe one morning you'll just happen to find yourself pregnant. Then all these doubts will start to fade away. Because you'll just know what to do."

"Is it as simple as that?" Kate asked. "I feel this urge to not trust my instincts—because that would be selfish."

"Oh Kate," Eileen said, "when they sold us on having it all, they neglected to highlight that we already had something incredibly profound within us. But we do. The one thing we can do that men cannot is give birth and be mothers. It's a gift from God to us—and our gift to the world."

Kate sighed. "I get it but, how were you able to manage your incredible career at the same time?"

"First and foremost, Chinese culture values family very much. And try as we might, you can't always outrun where you come from. But another thing. At times this political game forces you to act hard as nails.

And as a woman competing in a male-dominated arena, I sometimes come off as aggressive and biting. I get it, that's the nature of the business."

Eileen smiled. She said, "But I still remember changing my daughter's diapers and rocking her to sleep. That really puts things in perspective. And in four years, when this is all over for me, I envision stepping off Marine One and lifting my future grandchild into my arms. *That* is how I plan to spend my retirement, not waving banners in the streets."

"You'd walk away completely into private life?" Kate asked. "I don't know if I could do that."

"Well, I'm sure I'll give speeches and make other appearances as required of an ex-president, but the point is this. Even if you did want everything that you've gone after so far, you owe it to yourself to make sure that in another ten years, your life looks like what you want it to be."

"I will think about it, thank you."

After a silent moment, the president looked at her watch. "Hmm, they are taking their sweet time in there. Maybe a couple Dominguez supporters are on set."

Kate half-smiled, then said, "Eileen, do you ever have doubts about what we're doing?"

"You're always taking flak in my line of work, so you tend to question yourself as a matter of course. But more specifically, what's on your mind?"

"I mean, do you have any fears about the consequences of Reparations? What things will look like at the end?"

Jeffries-Lao exhaled. "If you're asking whether I feared that the database would turn into a surveillance state nightmare, I'll say this. While I was made aware that our project leader had left under protest, I guess you could say we were all swept up at the time envisioning the United States as just the first of many lanes on the Reparations highway. Obviously, things are a little dicey right now. But I've already dealt with a lot of naysayers this month, so please don't tell me you're also in that camp."

"I'd be lying if I said I didn't have any doubts," Kate said. "But I've been fighting for this cause for a long time. No one should doubt my commitment, but maybe they shouldn't ignore my concerns either."

"Well, you've got my ear while we're waiting. What scares you the most and what can we do to address it?"

"For one, I... We'd all be devastated if you lost next week."

"Not going to happen," Eileen said, "so cheer up. Next?"

"I think it's clear that the grace period is over for the HRA. We need to show people that they can still count on us."

"Six months from now, when we've tightened all the leaks and done a PR blitz about our commitment to privacy, I assure you this whole situation will be looked back upon as nothing more than growing pains."

"I do hope you're right." Kate paused, then said, "Since I have intimate HRA knowledge, would you be offended if I voiced another concern?"

"Not at all, Kate. You are an industry professional and I welcome your insights."

"Thank you. The impression I'm getting—from a few close colleagues, as well as how adamant the masked man was about even law enforcement losing faith in some of our more punitive methods—it seems as if internal fixes and PR blasts might not be enough to contain anti-Reparations sentiment."

"That's a valid fear," Eileen said. "I don't think

stricter methods to keep people in line are the answer."

"Especially if Telecom & Penal are able to get Congress to authorize their plans."

The president shook her head. "I'd almost forgotten about them. Turning our own database against us, terrible. Microscopic Protocol would do incalculable harm to the Beneficiary class."

"I know," Kate said wearily. "All of us at the HRA dread what a setback it could be."

"After the inauguration, my people will put as much pressure on them as possible to get them to reconsider taking that step."

"Thank you for hearing me out. All I want is to help the HRA in any way that I can. No doubt your administration has been under more pressure than I have since the hack, but... I'm really struggling to digest the public humiliation they put me through."

"Like it or not," the president said, "you're a public figure now. It can really be rough. Me? I've taken abuse for over twenty years from small town op-ed writers, foreign leaders, and of course those trolls in the meme brigade. But hopefully being in this ad with me will serve to rehabilitate your reputation—and help you get your confidence back."

"I appreciate your saying that," Kate said. "And because I admire you as such a strong woman, please allow me one last question."

"Of course."

"I thought I knew exactly who I was for the longest time. I believed in myself and was firing on all cylinders. But what that masked man said knocked my feet right out from under me. Every day since then has been a struggle."

"He really got into your head, didn't he?" The president shook her head with concern.

"I'm afraid so."

"Kate, in a few minutes I want you to step in front of that camera and envision that you're talking directly to him. Show that SOB he hasn't broken you and that you're stronger than ever. Because look, you're working with the President of the United States right now. And who's he? Just another disgruntled Debtor with no other way for his voice to be heard than by resorting to Ted Kaczynski tactics. Let's go show him who's boss!"

They finished shortly after five o'clock. Both were worn out after dozens of takes under bright lights. As they parted, the president offered Kate a few last kind words and a gentle hug. Kate left the building feeling a warm glow of satisfaction, and she couldn't wait to get home to celebrate with Chris.

But halfway through the subway ride, she remembered that he already had evening plans. Glenn, the singer from his old band, was in town and they were going out drinking. She was almost tempted to try and track them down once she got back to Brooklyn, but decided not to interrupt. Plus, she and Glenn weren't on the best terms these days…

Instead, Kate dropped by the neighborhood Whole Foods and treated herself to wine, cheese, and snacks. She was going to make the best of having to fly solo, because not everyone got to speak privately with the president for nearly half an hour—let alone become "fast friends," as Kate allowed herself to indulge.

She set up shop on the couch and opened the first bottle of a Peruvian Malbec. The dogs were attracted by the cheese and settled in around her. She was munching on pita chips and browsing maternity websites on the big screen, when suddenly she heard the chilling croak of her inner voice for the first time since her illness last summer.

"*Kaaaaaate,*" it said. "What are you thinking about? Don't tell me you're veering off course."

"Excuse me," Kate replied, "but the president of our country just gave me some very heartfelt advice. I'd be a fool—and ungrateful—not to think it over."

"But who are you to her? She doesn't know you, so why should she open up to you like that?"

"Probably because I and people like me were the ones who made her presidency possible. By the way, I just looked it up and she did in fact decline to run for re-election in California back in 'twenty-two. It was only because of the groundswell we created that she entered the presidential primaries."

"Nonsense! That may be a nice cover story, but as I recall, her campaign hit the ground running early in 'twenty-three. Maybe she was just buttering you up so you'd perform well on camera. Or, perhaps she was feeling you out for a potential job in her next administration. In which case..."

"Oh, you are a fiend! But that *would* be nice. Live and work close to my parents. But how would Chris feel? I guess, in theory, he could run his business from anywhere..."

"Bah, Chris. He's not really doing anything. Just a techie. You're out there making a difference!"

"Everyone needs support staff. I wasn't part of the construction crew that built my field office. And I don't know anything about the networks we run."

"But you *are* the one the HRA puts on TV."

"Be quiet! You're getting me all mixed up."

"Why won't you just trust me?" the voice cooed.

"Because I really need to know how much of me is not genuine, but something... else. I need to figure out where my life is going."

"But you've done so well on this track. First, you broke through the natural resistance and became aware of your privilege. And then you actually put this truth into action, changing millions of lives for the better in the process."

"All this talk about change, it's making me dizzy. Changing the world. Being a change agent. But who decides which changes are good? Are some people not fit to change anything?"

"Kate, my darling. I've known you for a long, long time. So permit me to speak freely here. The fact that you are so privileged is the very reason that you're equipped to bring about the better world we wish to see."

"Stop! Ugh—that phrase… 'Better world we wish to see.' My whole head is just filled with these canned lines. And they come from the likes of you!"

"Don't get mad at me! All this time, did you ever do anything you didn't want to? Did you not think highly of yourself after every canned food drive, charity run, and HRA outreach? You sure had a lot of fun for someone who claimed to be sacrificing for others."

"Wait a minute! That's what you're for. And haven't you been doing that since the beginning? Clicking the rows of the abacus back and forth to make sure it all evened out?"

"I tried. But no matter what I did, somehow I just couldn't keep up with your pride. The satisfaction you got from it all. That is *not* what this belief system is all about."

"What belief system? You make it sound like I joined a religious group. No way. This is supposed to be about the heart using the mind to help the less fortunate."

"Yes, but if you want to make a real impact, it can't

just be on an individual basis. You need a system to plug these ideas into. Hey, why the sour face? The HRA is that system—and you helped create it."

"I know what the HRA is, thank you very much. I'm sick to my stomach right now because I realize that schools are also part of a system that's designed in the same way, but nobody sees it. And I'm mad because I was never told what its real purpose was."

"Katie, don't turn your back on the strong women who set the stage for the trajectory of your life."

"But they did it without my permission! Would anyone send their children to a summer camp or a church, if they knew that the staff was going to subliminally put a secret ideology into their minds? Even if it's not criminal, it's not forthright—and nothing about how I've lived *my* life involves hiding the truth."

"Why do you want to pick things apart like this? After the fact? After all the good we've done—"

"We?! We? ... Oh my god... Who the hell are you anyway?"

"I—"

"Lurking in the back of my mind, always ready to pop out and throw in your two cents. It's funny, because everything you say boils down to me prostrating myself in order to... do what? Save the world? Well, you know, I'm tired. Exhausted, in fact. But I see it now. All these years, even when you were silent, you still pulled the strings. I just can't do it anymore. I'm done!"

"Kate, how can you say that? We've been working together for nearly fifteen years. I incubated in your mind, just like I was your baby, long before I even first spoke to you. We're one, together. You and me."

"No, no. I obeyed you because I trusted you. And

naturally, I *thought* you were my voice. But you're just an impostor! Someone slipped you into my subconscious, like an ideology roofie. They hijacked the direction of my entire life through you, and... and... now I'll crash this plane if that's what it takes to get free."

"Think twice before you do that, Kate. Without me, you'll just be out on a ledge, blind and alone. Stay with me, we can talk and work things out. You're a mature woman now, so maybe I can let go of the reins and give you more control. Heck, you've earned it. You've done far more than anything I could ever take credit for."

"What, are we bargaining now? About who gets what percentage stake of my mind? I'm not a company you can just divide up. This is *me!* And you are not my warden."

"No, I've never claimed to be in charge. If not a roommate, then maybe your spiritual guide? And now, yes, I can see that you're ready for more autonomy. But that doesn't mean you should just suddenly go out on your own. We have so much more work to do out there!"

"Have you not been paying attention to what's been going on lately? If not with the HRA, at least within me? I simply cannot move forward like before. I don't know what to do. ... Chris! The first thing I'm going to do is hold Chris in my arms and listen to what he's got to say. Poor guy, he's stood by me through everything so patiently, while *you* only keep nagging me and driving me forward with your whip."

"Oh, for God's sake. Chris, Chris... Damn him! That hypocrite. The little businessman hiding behind his punk rock t-shirts. What *do* you think is on his mind? While his wife was bounding around the country without him, chasing down a mystery that has led her right back into the gray matter inside her own head? Lost and found, Mrs. Kate Donohugh, thank you very much."

"You monster! Trying to poison me against my own husband. For what? So you can turn me into just another lonely old woman who's so bitter that no one is willing to put up with her?"

"Kate, stop right there. You really don't want to keep pulling that thread…"

"Or what? Will I find that there *is* something else in my mind? Something pure that you've been hiding? What is it? Where is it? You—get out of the way!"

"Kate, nooooo!"

Kate brought her hands up and cleared away a wash of tears that had filled her eyes. She reached for her phone and called Chris. It went directly to his voicemail.

"Hi, baby," she said softly, "it's me. I know you're out having fun tonight. I just want you to know that I love you so much. When I see you, I… I… Chris, I want you to be the father of our children."

11. THE WARNING

A burly man with a thick red beard carried a pitcher and two pint glasses away from the bar. He set them down in front of Chris Donohugh, then hung up his black satin flight jacket before sliding into the booth.

"Feels good to be back in Brooklyn," he said. "And it's great to see you again, man."

Chris poured the beer and then offered a toast. "Cheers, Glenn. Sucks we don't do this more often. Philly's not all that far away."

"Forget it, man. Life gets busy. I'm just glad you could meet up. Nice to have a day off before we hit the road again."

"You should've told me about the gig last night. Maybe I could have made it."

"Nah. Some dive up in the Bronx. I knew it was gonna be shit. I wanted to see you when I was in a good mood. Better mood, at least." Glenn gulped some beer and laughed. "So how you been? I see Kate's famous now."

"Yeah," Chris said. "Our dirty laundry aired out for

the world to see. Just awesome."

"Don't sweat it. That stuff passes. Who doesn't have something embarrassing as hell out there?"

"What's really insane is that after all that, somehow *the* president actually wanted Kate to be in a campaign commercial with her."

"Say what?!" Glenn called out.

"Oh yeah, no biggie," Chris said. "Jeffries-Lao's people just called her right up on Saturday."

"Haha, that's wild."

"Kate was tap dancing around the apartment all weekend. Anyway, the filming was supposed to happen today but I don't know how it went. Sometimes this shit's just too much, you know?"

"And that's why we drink!" Glenn said. "Well… In Chris news, are you still designing?"

"I can't stop. That's what keeps me out of the cubicle."

"I never liked offices either. Unless I've got a microphone in my hand, I'll stick to the shadows. Blue collar or bust, baby! Here, tilt your glass."

"Hold on," Chris said. "Let me pound this."

"That's my boy." Glenn's eyes moved to the TVs that were on the wall behind the pool tables. "Would ya look at that. A special news report about the Sentinels. 'Reparations on the Razor's Edge.' So dramatic! What do you think's gonna happen, Donohugh?"

Chris shrugged. "They'll get it squared away. It's too big of a deal to give up on. Like they say, these things only come around once every five hundred years, right?"

"Well, jeez. Lucky timing for us to live through it!" Glenn paused. "But check this out. You remember my ex, Jen?"

"Of course, man."

"Back when she was getting her PhD in women's studies, she was obsessed with this author Doris Lessing. Jen said her voice gave... let me try to remember this... 'a penetrating view into the ripples of colonialism throughout the twentieth century.' Such a scholar, I know.

"Anyway," he continued, "one time she came home with a box full of books—she'd bought someone's entire collection of Lessing's stuff. Turns out some of them were actually sci-fi. Jen didn't care but I was actually intrigued. I wanted to know what would compel such a famous author to switch gears like that. So I checked out the first book, *Shikasta*. It's dense, real slow going, but I gotta tell ya—there's *a lot* of real-world politics behind the space and aliens stuff. Like at one point, the survivors of World War Three decide to symbolically put the white race on trial for all its crimes."

"What the hell?" Chris said. "I never heard about any of this before. When was it written?"

"Dude, this series came out back around 1980."

"Holy shit! So what happens at the trial?"

Glenn said, "The delegates from around the world give their damning testimony. But then, just before the guilty verdict, the group from India steps up. And they have to admit that they treated their own Untouchable class like dirt for thousands of years—way longer than any Caucs were out there colonizing."

"Damn," Chris said. "Maybe no one *wants* to know about this book."

"Ha, you might be right."

"So did Jen read it after you told her about that scene?"

"Nope!" Glenn leaned back and exhaled. "And you know something else? The reason she and I broke up is because I didn't support Reparations one hundred and ten percent. Ain't that something?"

"Really?" Chris shook his head.

"Yeah. When everyone was getting fitted for halos as the whole thing ramped up, I had this uneasy feeling and just couldn't play along. I mean, I liked some of the ideas, but that wasn't enough for her. So one day she just ended it."

"Goddamn."

"It's alright," Glenn said. "I'm always thinking about stuff too much. And sorry I couldn't share this with you at the time. But you were married, living the normal life. And Kate was right there in the middle of it. I didn't need to be told by you that I was the weird one. Or have your wife cut me out of your life completely— which has sort of happened anyway, go figure."

"Oh man, Glenn," Chris said. "You've been my brother since we were in sixth grade. I don't give a shit what you think about the HRA. Now I'm just bummed you felt like you couldn't tell me what went down in your life."

"Don't sweat it, man. That's just how it goes. Relationship truths—some doors open, some slam shut. But tell me," Glenn added, leaning in, "now that we're buzzed and you're a free man for one night, what do you really think about Reparations?"

Chris chuckled. "It's been my policy for a long time to not even think about it at all. That helps keep the peace at home. I just focus on running my business."

"Ah, well played. The diplomat hunched over a fireplace blowing on embers to keep his indie spirit alive. But hey, with all those quotas promoting everybody else, I guess that makes you the odd man out anyway."

"Damn," Chris said. "That was a cheap shot."

"Nah. That's just the fallout from everything we fought for. A leg up for the marginalized, right? You were fine with putting that in our music, but then what happened? Didn't you ever want to work for them? And before you answer, understand that I am *not* judging you here."

"Whew. Things are getting heavy right now. But, going back to your original question—the part of my brain that didn't think about Reparations, it finally has recently. And I even told Kate some of this, so don't think I'm being a coward or a hypocrite here."

"And how did she react?" Glenn asked.

"Hold on. First, I think they opened up Pandora's Freakin' Box and it could spiral out of control into a big mess."

"I knew it all along! But no one listens to Glenn, 'cause I'm an asshole."

"Yeah, yeah," Chris said. "Look, all the surveillance tools are getting smarter and smaller. The reach back into history is gonna go so damn far beyond 1492, I can't even comprehend what the impact will be."

"Just domino after domino falling down." Glenn drained his glass. "The HRA got through the first couple innings with no sweat, but the rest of this game is gonna be a nail-biter. Lawsuits. Petitions for exemption. And here's my big thing I'm waiting for. What if someone finds a document that ends up knocking the whole timeline out of whack? Revisionist historians will have a field day! Think total narrative collapse, bro."

"Not sure I follow you, to be honest."

"Remember the ending of *Raiders of the Lost Ark*? All those artifacts just getting locked away forever? Talk about inconvenient archives! If they get Reparations going in other countries, we're talking maybe a million scanners around the world. Who knows what some shaman up in the hills might submit? Unless a narrative safeguard gets programmed into MARVIN, just one obscure scrap of paper could force us to rewrite world history. Then who do you send the monthly bill to?"

"So if something like that happens, where they have to change the timeline… What would the HRA do?"

Glenn said, "I have no clue. The bigger point is that the program has such a narrow focus, they forgot how complicated everything really is. How do you help one group without hurting another if you frame everything as a zero-sum game? Holding whites up as the all-time evildoers doesn't leave much room for reconciliation."

"You know," Chris said, "I find it almost impossible to believe that the guy who wrote the song 'God of Exploitation' is now saying all this. What the hell pushed you so far in the other direction?"

Glenn fidgeted with his beer glass.

He said, "It started with my dad. He's been sick. His hip and his back are messed up too, so he's laid up most of the time. And what's on the TV? Sitcoms and news anchors saying how great Reparations is. He busted his ass on job sites to put food on the table for me and my brother. Now he's fading away with crap healthcare— but the HRA still takes its cut every month! Not much dignity in all that."

Chris frowned. "Sorry he's having a tough time. Your dad was always a great guy to be around. And a big help to the band when we needed support. But… we all have to pay. I just don't see what he's got to do with this Reparations talk."

"Listen to me, Chris. He's going to his grave with a new kind of bitterness that wasn't there five years ago. And if it's happening to him, it's happening to other white people too. So you know, take their money, whatever. They've been feeding that bottomless pit of taxes their whole life. But now, you want to dig up all this dirt and back them into a corner with accusations? Maybe haul them off to a debtors' prison, or make them have a Kumbaya moment on TV like Kate got dragged into?

"I'm telling you," Glenn added, "it's no good. You're draining decent people of their compassion and replacing it with some ice-cold shit. And here's what keeps me up at night. If what the big narrative says is true, then they took over the whole world once already. Put them in a cage and start poking them out of revenge—be careful you don't reawaken that European bloodlust that's been dormant since the end of World War Two."

Chris shivered. "You're scaring the hell out of me, man. That's some Nazi-level shit. Do I have to quote another one of your songs?"

"That's not even the point!" Glenn said. "You join a band when you're young and the scene provides the wardrobe and all the cookie-cutter song topics. Punk, metal... Everything's all laid out there for you. So of course we sang about evil skinheads, workers' rights, anti-war stuff—we covered all the bases. But I never wrote a song about Mao and he killed a lot of people, that's for damn sure. So yeah, let's go hook up MARVIN in China and see what he has to say about all that!"

"Nah, come on," Chris said. "Don't get too wasted now. You were making an actual point about your dad."

"Alright, alright. Look. How much frustration or outright failure do you have to go through in life, before maybe you start to drop parts of this worldview that we swallowed at age what, fourteen?"

"I don't know, you tell me."

"If our stupid band hadn't had even the minor level of success that it did, we would've been forced to face these facts in our early twenties. But as it is—"

"Hold on, dude!" Chris protested. "One, don't throw Raucous Voice under the bus. And two, I've been running this tech business for eight years. You're the one still playing in bands, banging sluts, and chasing the dream. But *now* that you're finally discovering reality, you want to show it to *me?* I'm the married guy! I'm always in check."

Glenn sighed. "I'm not trying to get holier than thou on you, bud. And maybe in some ways I am behind the curve compared to you. But I see the big picture really clearly right now. When I look at my father's face, lying on that couch... I just wonder how many able-bodied white guys have stopped engaging on social media because they believe the time for conversation is over. Do you want to see them get violent?"

"Hell no," Chris said.

"Neither do I. Nobody does." Glenn paused. "So maybe it's a good thing that the Sentinels of Jubilee are out there, assuming they really do want to keep everything peaceful. And maybe because they've got momentum, that's why the revolutionary types are hanging back. But what if the cops find their leaders and drag them in front of the cameras?"

"Jesus. You think they'd rise up and trash some cities?"

"I think... that I don't know who I want to win this election. Because if she does, will that push these guys over the edge? But if Dominguez wins, maybe the HRA falls apart so fast that it's the Bennies who do the shooting."

Chris dropped his head into his hands. "How did we get here? It's like overnight it all just changed."

Glenn poured out the last of the pitcher into their glasses.

He said, "There was one big, old problem that we tried to face, but the plan was so one-dimensional that it didn't consider all the other little problems too. I think the real mistake was taking a good policy, like high taxes for the rich, and trying to morph it by saying, 'Oh, since you're white you have privilege, which is a *kind* of wealth, so we can take that too.'

"But," Glenn continued, "people still have mortgages, old cars, and even bands that want to rehearse but can't afford to, because the money they would have set aside for a new PA system got sucked up by the HRA. But I'm the bad guy now for making it personal."

"I see what you're saying," Chris said. "They're picking and choosing between people's dreams."

"Exactly. And now they can't put the genie back in the bottle. Spent billions on the HRA infrastructure. Moved trillions of dollars around. That's why maybe the Sentinels have the right idea in calling for some sort of transition out."

"You've mentioned them a few times now. They convinced you, just like that?"

"Bear with me. The HRA has hundreds of locations around the country. Tens of thousands of scanners all over the place. Why not make use of it all in other ways? Like, let's encourage people to submit their poetry or paintings to a national cultural database. Then we can sit in awe of everyone's creativity, whatever their race or gender."

"Okay," Chris said, "I like that…"

"Next, repurpose the HRA branches so that instead

of splitting people into two groups, it's a welcoming place for charity and volunteer work. Just like we used to do at the soup kitchens back in the day—we wanted to be there, and the people appreciated our help."

"Yeah, make it a two-way street. But will enough volunteers show up? I mean, probably one reason we needed the HRA was because the resources weren't there."

"I don't know," Glenn said. "But is it wrong to think that after a few years of testing this huge program, we might want to take some readings and course correct if necessary?"

"That sounds a lot better than going on TV in a friggin' mask and scaring the shit out of everybody."

"Maybe people needed a wake-up call. Because maybe a thousand guys like me carefully explaining this kind of pivot would fall on deaf ears. Maybe it already has."

Chris said, "Are you dancing around something here? If you've got something else to say, spit it out."

"I want to," Glenn said. "I just don't know if you, because of the position you're in, can really handle it."

"What does that mean, 'my position'?"

"It means your wife damned near took a pledge of allegiance to serve Reparations! And I love you too much to risk putting anything between you and Kate unless your eyes are open."

"Yeah, my wife," Chris said. "Who went on some spiritual quest and has barely said a damn thing about it since she came back. My wife, who I stood by when she got sick and was nearly losing her mind. So just say it, man."

Glenn said, "Let's take a walk. I've got to tell you some stuff and we shouldn't be surrounded by people when I do it."

They finished their beers and walked out to a side street.

"Okay," Glenn said. "Let's assume the techs get MARVIN debugged and back online. How do I say this? I mean, you're a computer guy. Have you not heard the rumors that this religious guy the Prescient One is actually MARVIN's original designer?"

"That nut job covered in glitter?" Chris said. "I don't know. Sounds like just a good cover story to get people to join his cult."

"No, Chris. It's true. He designed the whole system that Kate and her coworkers use every day. But— there's more, and I swear to God I'll kill you if you go behind my back—"

"Jesus Christ! What's got you so edgy? I'm your bro, tell me what's up?"

Glenn put his lips to Chris's ear and whispered, "The masked man *is* the Prescient One."

"Holy shit…"

"I've been working with the underground for a while. Sometimes we share information with the Sentinels. And now you're going to help us."

Chris slowly pulled away and ran his hands through his hair. "So this wasn't a chance meeting at all. You didn't just happen to be passing through New York."

"We were on the road, man. The shows were booked. Why wouldn't I look up an old friend on our night off? I was gonna find a way to connect with you, one way or another, when the time was right."

"Yeah, sure. Look, I don't know what you're planning to say here. All I can promise is to listen. And short of murder, I won't give you away. Now, what do you want from me?"

"Let's hit another bar first," Glenn said. "You're gonna need a stiff drink."

Chris walked Glenn to the subway entrance, sending off the friend he'd known for twenty years with a firm embrace. It was good to know that Glenn, even if he tended to shoot from the hip, was loyal and spoke from the heart.

Chris looked at his phone during the cab ride and saw that he had a voicemail from Kate. Between the haze of alcohol and trying to process all that had been discussed with Glenn, hearing her message put his mind over its daily limit and he went blank the rest of the way home.

It was nearly one o'clock when the cab dropped him off. He entered the apartment as quietly as he could. A metal jangling sound came from the living room, then light tapping along the hardwood floor. One of the Corgis rubbed against his legs in the darkness.

He crept down the hall and saw Kate sprawled out on the couch. The other dog was asleep next to her head. Two wine bottles, one empty and one half full, sat on the coffee table.

Kate was breathing easy. Chris studied the contours of her pale face. A strand of dirty-blond hair had fallen across her chin.

He leaned over carefully and picked up her wine glass, then poured himself a small drink. He sat down at the end of the couch and leaned back. The dog that had met him at the door now came over and lay down at his feet.

Chris thought about how life was crazy and confusing and you never knew what was coming next. But life was also good. He drained the glass and set it down, then rested his hand on Kate's ankle.

He was soon fast asleep.

12. THE ASSIGNMENT

Elder Evans jerked awake. He sat up and turned on the bedside lamp. Two elite guards stood above him in this small private room, which he had moved into after the advancement ceremony a week ago.

"What are you doing in here?" he asked. "What do you want?"

"Pack your things," one of the guards said.

"Why? What's happening? Am I being evicted from the church?"

The guards laughed. "You're going for a ride on TP-One. Now get ready. The helicopter leaves in twenty minutes."

Elder Evans gathered his few possessions and stuffed them into a duffle bag. He hastily freshened up then presented himself to the guards, who were waiting outside in the hallway.

They escorted him down several corridors which were vacant at this early hour, then across a walkway where the night's subtle glow came in through the skylights. The trio next passed through a guarded door, and soon came to an elevator. One of the guards waved a key card and it opened. They rode to the top floor, then after exiting walked down a ramp toward sliding glass doors.

Elder Evans saw a jet black helicopter sitting on the rooftop. As he and the guards approached, the Prescient One stepped out.

"Here he is, sir," a guard said.

"Wonderful, wonderful." The Prescient One put his arm around Elder Evans and whispered, "Good morning, Elder. How are you?"

"They put the fear of Mod in me waking me up like that. I thought for a moment that I'd been found out."

"Nothing of the sort! And now, as we step on board, you will cease to be Bill Evans. Are you ready to go to Iowa, Marcus?"

"I have all my belongings with me. I am at your service."

"Bless you." The Prescient One waved to the guard standing just outside the door. "We're ready. Prepare for departure."

The guard boarded and closed the door. He put on a headset and said, "Captain, we're ready to go. Take this bird up."

The flight had been a quiet one. Shortly after leaving the Mall, the Prescient One covered his face with the hood of his cloak and dozed off. Marcus soon fell asleep as well. A while later, as the sun began to peek above the horizon, he awoke and saw the Prescient One staring at him.

"How does it feel to be an elder?"

"It's an honor to be in that position of trust," Marcus said.

"I must say, I very much enjoyed your cover story

for Bill. The 'peeping Tom who stole my wife' tale, perfect! But that's not you at all, and eventually you couldn't hide it."

"I guess not."

"Scholar-athlete," the Prescient One said. "Son of an attorney and a CEO. The sky seemed to be the limit for you. So I must ask, what motivated you to join a branch of law enforcement?"

"I grew up around people who had a lot of money," Marcus said. "But that didn't necessarily make their kids smart or even honorable. At first I pursued a law degree because I was intrigued by how rules, that were supposedly set in stone, became subjected to endless interpretation in cases that involved real people."

"Fascinating. And yet you didn't end up working in offices."

"I realized I was too young to be cooped up like that. I had to get out into the field and put all of my skills to use."

"Ah, so by the time you came to our church, it was just another assignment for you?"

"Yes," Marcus said. "The point of the mission was to keep an eye on this crazy new church that had come out of nowhere and was growing so quickly. We didn't want another Jim Jones to happen on our watch."

"But instead, we found our way into your heart."

Marcus smiled. "I let my guard down. Didn't keep my distance."

"It could happen to anyone." The Prescient One waved a hand. "We're all so used to the frantic pace of life in the outside world, that we have no frame of reference that something could be wrong. And I'm well aware of how ironic it is that people need to experience *my* church to get a taste of normalcy."

"Yes, it's quite the paradox. May I ask, how many

of my church colleagues and superiors know of my true identity?"

"The emissaries are aware of almost everything that goes on at the Mall. They're the real security force, not the armed guards and plainclothes lookouts that we regrettably must employ. You see, Marcus, the truth is that you are far from being the only spy within our walls. I would say that at any given time, perhaps two percent of Mall residents are there on behalf of some other group, and not actually following their own hearts."

Marcus said, "I suspected a few people from time to time. What normally happens to them when they're caught?"

"It depends what their agenda is. Sometimes they're harmless. Sometimes we can make use of them. But sometimes…"

"You have to kill them?"

"Oh, not at all!" the church leader said. "We may forcibly remove them, yes. But besides the occasional fisticuffs, the worst we ever do is more of a prank. We knock them out with a laced drink, then leave them in a field somewhere not far from a gas station or convenience store. They wake up to find that their whole body has been painted blue! But the best part is, we also spray silver glitter onto their skin through stencils with the words, 'Mod bless you!' They rarely bother us again."

Marcus raised his eyebrows. "You've been an interesting study, sir."

"As have you," the Prescient One said with a wink.

"On the one hand, you're deadly serious and forward-thinking. But on the other, this silliness and playfulness… I can't quite put my finger on it."

The Prescient One leaned in. "Why aren't you

married, Marcus?"

Marcus turned his gaze toward the window, then down. "I'd say commitment to my career was more important. Setting myself up on the right path would give me better marriage prospects down the road."

"But you're nearly forty now. Surely you're well enough along that path?"

"The last six years I've been embedded undercover more than half of the time. Hard to start something meaningful under those circumstances, let alone keep it going."

"Indeed. And you did not meet any women that you fancied during your time with us?"

"That's not true," Marcus said. "There are two I was fond of, in fact. But I had to stay focused on my mission for the FBI. Plus, the rules regarding courtship, Modestianity's whole approach to sexuality…"

"So natural as to be confusing for the twenty-first-century mind, perhaps?" The Prescient One smiled softly.

Marcus said, "I remember once writing in my diary the phrase 'druidic chivalry' to describe it. I admit that there's something genius in your approach. Like a spigot—there's a time and a place to turn it on and water the plants. But then you keep it shut tight and focus on the other aspects of life."

"Well said. We've been so saturated with sex in our culture that we lost all sense of its purpose. Putting it in ads to sell products. Being able to view any act imaginable from the safety of an office chair—it's perversion through the looking glass. Because this almost clinical distance made us forget that we *are* animals, and that sex is the most primal, non-intellectual part of our being. Too much and we lose ourselves. Too little and we fall into neurosis."

"You've got it all so thought out," Marcus said. "Somehow every aspect of Modestianity is ready to fill the needs of people living in this modern world. But so much of its core draws from ancient models of human behavior. How did this harmonious philosophy form so quickly? Did it just appear to you in a dream?"

The Prescient One ran his fingers down the side of his face, where today he wore a partial mask of crescent-shaped molded plastic that ran along the jawline.

"It's hard to take credit for something that you created in a state of desperation," he said. "Or horror. For you see, when I looked deep into MARVIN's eyes, I saw the nightmarish future in a flash. A time when good people armed with this technology would terrorize each other, not for justice, but to pillage and defame. Creation, discovery, culture—all would stop dead in their tracks.

"Had I not been abruptly cast out of the HRA," he continued, "perhaps we could have built some safeguards into the system. Yes, it would have lacked the comprehensive depth that Modestianity now possesses, but it would have had a much wider influence."

"But that's not how it played out," Marcus said.

"No. I was forced into exile. Had my Moses moment out in Colorado. Then I began the humble task of preaching in the streets, trying to save the souls of people busily rushing from swipe to swipe. But with every speech I became more confident in myself. And soon, people started to resonate with my words because what I saw removed the cataracts from their souls!

"They were trapped in the paradox of having gorged on every piece of information, every TV show, every type of food, and yet were still spiritually starved. That, my friend, was the true key to Modestianity's rise. You can only bring so many people into your church with scare tactics. But to keep them, you must offer them a hopeful alternative to their malaise."

"It works." Marcus shrugged his shoulders. "It worked on me."

The Prescient One's contact lenses twinkled blue. "I know."

"I kept my defenses up against the ladies that I admired, never realizing that Modestianity was also working its charms. Maybe my superiors will say that I have Stockholm Syndrome."

"Nonsense," the sage replied. "If you discard my ornamentation and eccentric ways, what you're left with is an approach toward life which denies less of our human essence than other religions. Modestianity seeks to draw out the best from each, for each. Thankfully, my wealth kept us uncompromised during the first years, and now the acolytes who emanate joy and satisfaction in their local churches are the best recruiting tool we have."

"Your Prescience," Marcus said, "I don't know why you specifically called on me today, but I assume that I have passed a test of character. Would I be too presumptuous in daring to ask a personal question?"

"Not at all, Elder."

"You asked me about not being married," Marcus began. "I figure we must be close in age. And yet I don't see you with a queen on stage. There hasn't even been gossip about you taking advantage of any of the female novitiates. You have so much power and a glorious title, yet your reputation remains spotless. How can this be?"

"Think of a mountain climber," the Prescient One

said. "He sets out along a trail, scales the first wall, then continues hiking until the next climb. Up and up he goes, steadily onward. Do you think he will just stop and turn around before he reaches the summit?"

"No."

"So it has been for me. And like the climber exploring new areas where the terrain has not been mapped out, I never knew that after each success there could be an even higher peak behind it. Most game developers in my position after a triumph like *Thor's Tablet* would have moved laterally within the industry. But then I saw great potential in the blockchain movement, so I focused completely on that new field of interest. It too was another massive success.

"And when the HRA planners came to me," the Prescient One added, "it was a fresh challenge to surmount. While working on such an important program, I simply could not let myself be distracted or I might fall."

"But something did snap your rope anyway," Marcus said.

"Or maybe it saved me. Because while licking my wounds, I saw a glorious new mountain in an undiscovered country. And I have been climbing this tallest peak ever since, while also serving as guide for countless other climbers. Until we reach the top, how can I commit to a marriage? Too much of humanity's fate is on the precipice.

"I now see," the Prescient One said, "that everything I have done and endured in life prepared me to lead people out of their despair. And after one terrible fall from grace, I cannot allow even the slightest hint of an allegation of impropriety against me, not when the stakes are so much higher."

"But other powerful men have had wives," Marcus

offered. "Presidents, generals, religious leaders. Is your mission really more important than theirs?"

"Marcus, I value your concerns. Have you noticed that many people are being promoted to higher office throughout the church? These are the next wave of visionaries who will enrich Modestianity, because soon I will step out into the world to unveil an even greater plank of my vision."

"What?!"

"Yes, it's true," the Prescient One said. "I will not linger in the Mall like some god to be worshiped, not if Modestianity is truly is about the people and not me."

"You're going to leave us?" Marcus pleaded. "And do what?"

"Please calm yourself, dear Elder. You are still so new to this. The only way I can describe the next frontier is by calling it, prescience beyond prescience. But until that day, there is still crucial work to do. And you are an essential part of these plans. Will you honor me by serving in good faith?"

Marcus said, "You know very well I've thrown in my lot with Modestianity. All I hope is that the FBI doesn't come down too hard on me—or the church."

"Never mind that for the moment. Ah, we're almost there." The Prescient One pointed to a cluster of buildings sitting within a sea of cropland. "The church's charter is expanding, Marcus. Beyond souls and identities. We must conduct humanitarian missions for those in need."

"Where are we?" Marcus asked.

As the helicopter eased down into a patch of cut grass within a larger field, the Prescient One said, "I call it the Farm."

They were greeted by a staff of fifteen. A cook, a groundskeeper, two doctors, three guards, and the rest nurses. Marcus remained silent while they toured the grounds. The Prescient One asked the staff members questions about various aspects of the facility.

There was one large building, which was surrounded by a spacious yard, two smaller buildings, several gardens, a horse enclosure, a work shed, and a barn. Inside the main building was a dining hall, small private bedrooms, a crafts room, and an entertainment and gaming hall.

Finally Marcus could hold his tongue no longer and quietly said, "What is this place, Your Prescience?"

The Prescient One walked to a large front window and smiled. "It looks like they're here."

Marcus followed as the staff walked out the front entrance and lined up in the yard. A convoy of six vehicles was coming up the drive.

"This is just the beginning," the Prescient One whispered to Marcus, "of a very important new phase of our mission. It is my honor to place you in charge of this test run."

"But who's in those vans? What am I overseeing exactly?"

"Just wait. You'll soon understand."

The white vehicles swung around in front of the group and stopped. Orderlies got out and opened the side and rear doors.

A hulking black man in desert camo who only had one arm stepped out of the first van. He turned back and offered his hand to a tired-looking white man with unkempt hair, who then limped out onto the grass.

Other men wearing various styles of military fatigues also exited the vehicles. They too showed signs of either injury or ill health. After they had all gotten out, one of the men yelled, "Attention!" They fell into place and stood tall.

The Prescient One came forward, his blue cloak fluttering in the light morning breeze.

"Gentlemen, I hope your journey was comfortable. Welcome to the Farm!"

As most of the group nodded, the man with the wild hair nudged the one-armed man and said quietly, "Would you take a look at this guy?"

"I know! I still got the blues for you," the other man sang. They both started laughing.

The Prescient One turned toward them. "Is something the matter?"

The white man waved a hand while they both tried to cover their faces.

"Oh," the Prescient One said, "is this not James Haggerston? Yes, I do believe it is. The fugitive from justice!"

James got serious and took a step back. "Wait a sec. Is this all some big trick? We were told that they were taking us somewhere to get real medical care."

"And this is it. The Sentinels never lie."

Marcus's jaw dropped. The Prescient One turned back to him and nodded with a smile. Marcus took a deep breath and regained his composure.

"Now, James," the Prescient One said, "I specifically requested your group of veterans. Do you have any idea why?"

"No, sir."

"I did so because I owe your son Morgan a debt of gratitude."

"Oh, my God!" James said. "You *are* the Prescient One. So he made it to the Mall safe?"

"Not only that, he showed great character as a faux-acolyte. And ultimately his words helped convince me to go on... my walkabout."

"Do you have a message from him? I was out in the

shanty towns helping round these other guys up for months. I haven't spoken to Morgan since the summer."

The Prescient One said, "I'm afraid he left the church grounds during my absence. I have no news. But please, introduce me to your friend with the wonderful singing voice."

James beamed. "This is Private First Class Bo Alexander. We served together during the First Gulf War back in 'ninety-one."

Bo extended his one hand—the left—and the Prescient One took it, saying, "Thank you for your service. I'm pleased to meet you."

"And thank you for the hospitality," Bo said. He elbowed James. "This fool found me and ten other guys killing time down in Texas. We just wanted to be left alone away from all the stupidity that's going on. But no, this old stiff, who claims he can barely text, he used the internet to track me down."

"Don't blame it all on me," James said. "The underground has these whiz kids that helped me out. Admit it, you were glad to see my face after all these years."

"You wish! Look at you, trying to get the band back together."

"We did have some times though. Then and now. Tell him about the drones we fought off!"

Bo said, "Mister TPO, get this. When we all left that shithole town heading for the barracks the Sentinels set up, some government drones attempted to engage us along the way."

"S'more Stoppers," James said. "But I've had experience with them. We took 'em out!"

"Fierce suckers, like giant flying beetles. But James is right. We won that skirmish. Then this cracker here, he made me take a picture of him with his foot on top of one. Like it was a hunting trophy!"

"But I had to!" James said. "One of them tasered me the last time. So yeah, I got my revenge."

"Anyway," Bo said, "looks like we're holding up this little ceremony. Excuse us."

The Prescient One smiled. "By all means. I'm glad you're here." He motioned for Marcus to step forward. "Gentlemen, this is Marcus Young. *Former* FBI undercover agent, current Modestian elder, and now the superintendent of this facility. Marcus, we've got two dozen men who have served their country honorably and are in need of treatment. Do you think you can handle that?"

Marcus said, "All the arrangements have been made, Your Prescience. Gentlemen, it will be a privilege to make your stay here as comfortable as possible. The staff will now see you to your rooms."

The Prescient One stood beside Marcus, and they watched the contingent of veterans slowly make its way into the main building. He said, "Life is truly sublime."

"How do you mean?" Marcus asked.

"You never know where it's going to take you. But as long as you fulfill what you're supposed to do each step of the way, you always end up in the right place."

Marcus folded his arms. "I've spent the last week joyfully immersing myself in my new role at the Mall. But you're saying I was meant to be all the way out here instead?"

"Marcus," the Prescient One sighed, "this is not exile. Nor is it your last stop. What we're doing here at the Farm is just the tip of the spear for where Modestianity will go in the future. I hope I wasn't wrong in selecting you for this task."

"No, Your Prescience." Marcus paused. "Forgive

me if you saw any disappointment in my face. It's just that, to go from betraying my government over a religious experience, to then being taken away from the life I would have led as an elder… I… I know that this is a profound opportunity to serve. Tonight I will pray for strength and guidance."

"Mod bless you. Keep the faith."

"Thank you. I shall strive to prove your prescient instincts correct."

As Marcus walked toward the door, he turned back to see the Prescient One smiling at the sun.

"…I still got the blues…"

13. AT THE CROSSROADS

It had been a few weeks since Clyde had spoken to Nolan in person. Nolan was busy traveling around meeting with community groups that had been impressed by his message during their *Nifty Minutes* appearance a month ago.

Clyde, meanwhile, had stayed local while trying to finish his new song. He worked for days on end writing and rewriting the lyrics, and slowly Eddie Pryor's offer began to weigh on his mind. The temptation to sign on to Hollywood's version of the big time butted up against his own desire to see if he could produce another relevant track. Did he really have talent, or was Eddie just trying to make a quick buck off a hot trend?

Nolan's schedule finally opened up so they could meet on Friday afternoon. Clyde loaded his phone with the beats and lyrics he had come up with so far, then hired a private car to take him over to Nolan's building. Clyde smiled at one point when they passed a local bus that was pulling over to the side of the road—it was nice not having to wait on the public transit schedule for rides anymore.

Once inside Nolan's building, Clyde rode up to the third floor and saw Damon waiting for him outside the elevator.

"Hey, DJC," Damon said. "Nice to see your face again."

"Sup, Dee?" Clyde said. "I can't believe y'all got eyeball scanners down in the lobby. Nolan do that?"

"We got to be careful nowadays. Lots of curious folks poking around our business."

"For a second it felt like I was walking into a bank or something."

"We makin' money, that's for sure."

"So, you Nolan's number one general now?"

Damon said, "Basically. I mean, I probably got moved up quicker because of all the action with your track. First off, Nolan been super busy giving them speeches all around. And then, some of the older guys didn't like the extra heat they was sensing around our operation. So they took off. That left me in a good spot."

"No doubt. You been able to handle all that?" Clyde asked.

"Aw man, at first it was a lot! But I learned to delegate like a champ. Follow me, I got to show you something."

Damon led Clyde down a hallway, then flashed a key card to unlock a door with a glass window. They walked into a darkened room where a half dozen boys were working at computer terminals. A couple of them glanced over before turning back to their screens.

"Welcome," Damon said, "to the bowels of our empire. You think I'm good with gadgets and tech? Hell no! These little brats can surf smarter, type faster, and post better than you or me. By a mile!"

"So what they doing in here?" Clyde said.

"Company business. Searching for talent. Maybe even promoting you."

"Oh, really?"

"Hey, yo!" Damon called out. "Don't any of you kids recognize DJ Clydoscope when he standing right in front of you?"

Again, only a few boys looked back and gave a wave before returning to their computers.

"See? They're machines! DJC is just another project for them. Let's get on out of here—these kids make me nervous sometimes."

"So," Clyde said, as they walked back down the hallway, "they just up here working all the time?"

"Yeah," Damon said. "Day and night. Never stop til they mama tell 'em to come home. Yo, one of them's even called *Ervin!*"

"Haha, that's too close for comfort."

"That's what I'm sayin'. Anyhow, what's up with you? We all still waitin' on your next song to drop."

"I know, I know," Clyde said. "I feel like I'm almost set on what it's gonna be, just want to get some perspective from Nolan before I pull the trigger."

"Good luck getting much time with him."

"I know! He's been so busy."

Damon said, "All this national exposure's got him pulled in different directions. I mean, no one expected y'all's song to blow up like it did. But anyhow, other folks payin' attention now too, like churches and schools. They all want Nolan to work with them, give speeches or whatever. I don't know what it means for me and what we doin' here."

"Yeah," Clyde said, "if the Pigeon Man goes straight, what happens to the old operation?"

"He don't like to be called that no more."

"What? Naw, he all about them birds!"

"Not anymore," Damon said. "We gettin' too big for that. So I'm just telling you—"

"Telling him what?" Nolan said angrily as he stepped off the elevator. He cracked a smile. "Clyde, come here and give me some love."

They came together for a quick hug and pat on the back.

"Let me look at you," Nolan said. "The world-famous Clyde Jenkins and he can't even grow sideburns."

"Get off me with that!" Clyde said, throwing a playful jab at Nolan's shoulder.

"When I was your age, I had a goatee and could bench press three hundred pounds. Look at both y'all, scrawny kids strong enough to lift a soda can and that's about it."

"And a microphone."

"Yeah, yeah. I'll believe that when I hear a second song from you, boy."

Clyde said, "That's kind of what I'm here to talk to you about."

"Alright. But run upstairs with me for a minute. I got to check on what these guys are doing."

Clyde and Nolan took the elevator to the top floor, then walked up a small flight of stairs that led out onto the roof. A ray of sunlight caught them in the eyes.

"Hmm," Clyde said. "Back where it all began."

"Don't get too nostalgic now," Nolan said. "We all still got work to do."

A few guys not much younger than Clyde were hacking at the planter boxes which Nolan used to hide the contraband HRA mini-drones that he'd bought and reprogrammed for his own uses.

"Keep going! Chop, chop!" Nolan called out as he

and Clyde walked past into the work shack.

Inside, a boy of ten wearing goggles was using a soldering iron to mangle the components of a small green motherboard. Once finished, he carefully set the hot tool in its holder, then closed the drone's plastic housing and manually tightened the hex screws.

Nolan flicked Clyde on the chest. "Got my *real* protege workin' in here decommissioning these drones."

"Oh yeah?" Clyde said. "Then what you plannin' to do with 'em?"

"Got to return these birds to their rightful owner. Government property and all. Especially now that we're trying to go more legit."

"So it really is rest in peace for the Pigeon Man, huh?"

"It's night, night for him. And hello, Mr. Simmons!"

Clyde stepped outside while Nolan conferred with the kid at the work bench. The guys over at the planters gave him a nod and a "wassup" before continuing to dismantle the wood boxes. A moment later Nolan came out of the shack and waved.

He said, "Let's go talk in my office like real businessmen."

They rode down to the fourth floor and Nolan keyed in to a huge room that Clyde vaguely remembered as being a lot smaller. It was filled with high-end production equipment—camera stands, a green screen, fancy desks, TVs, studio racks—and cardboard boxes were stacked all over the place.

"Hey," Clyde said, "what's all this? Are you building a real studio in here or what?"

"A little different this time around, isn't it?" Nolan said. "No expenses spared. Knocked down some walls, too. Gonna do this place up right. Home Base Studios,

I want to call it. Be an executive producer on a whole stable of projects. The mastermind behind the scenes, like Jerry Bruckheimer."

"What kind of stuff?" Clyde asked.

"First thing I want to do is get some news anchor types doing a weekly show talking about what's going on in our world. No pro sports talk or Middle East BS, just real life on the ground floor. But I'm so damn busy that I don't know when it's actually gonna happen. Also trying to wind down the old business—thinking about putting Damon in charge, but he ain't sure what he want to do. Go legit and be humble, or take the risk and be the big dog?"

"Looks like you really planning things out."

"Hey," Nolan said, "I got twenty years on you, kid. I'm late to the party compared to you, so I got to keep the pedal to the metal."

"Yeah, I'm at the big party for now." Clyde paused. "Just not sure I got what it takes to stay there."

"Why you say that?"

"It's this next song, man. I know what I want to do, what the message should be. But maybe ain't nobody gonna like it."

"Why's that?" Nolan asked. "You got to sing from the heart."

"That's what I thought too. But now it's like, the business people don't even care what you talk about. They'll run with your attitude no problem, long as you let 'em dress you up in some fashion designer's clothes."

"Nothing wrong with looking good. Why not take some of their gear?"

"I don't want to look like a clown!" Clyde said. "Who knows what they'd put on me?"

"I feel you." Nolan paused. "But set those guys

aside for right now. You got the hot mic, not them. What's on your mind?"

Clyde said, "I got a lot of different fans, Nolan."

"I know you do. In hoods all across the U-S-and-A."

"No, I mean different *kinds*. At this one club in Hollywood, a lot of white people came out to meet me. Just regular folks. And they were nice. Shook my hand. And not fake, like they was just happy to say hi and didn't want nothin' from me."

"So what's that mean to you?" Nolan asked.

"Feels like I'm trapped between two or three places," Clyde said. "See, my song let everybody know what's up with the HRA. But I did it because I wanted it to get better, not just fall apart and leave people with nothing."

"Yeah," Nolan said, "but 'technical difficulties beyond our control' and the hack are conspiring to try to bring down the HRA just the same."

"Mm-hmm. You got one side trying to cash in on my frustration and turn it into a brand. Another side is trying to use it like a soundtrack for their revolution. But there's also everyday people who got no agenda, no power—and they appreciate my song just for what it is."

"One small piece of powerful, political art."

Clyde blushed and looked down.

"But anyway, these people," he said, "they have their own minds, just like me. I can't forget about them just 'cause they're Caucs and we supposed to be mad, because of our ancestors or whatever. Especially if what the hackers say is true, then the real enemy ain't even human at all."

"MARVIN."

"Yeah," Clyde said. "Stupid name for the devil to have, too."

"Whatchu you talkin' about?" Nolan started wriggling his arms and body around wildly. "Hail MARVIN, yo! Oh Lord MARVIN, cast us not into the hard drive of hell!"

"Haha, you crazy. But that's a good line though. I may have to use it."

"On the house," Nolan said. "But keep going. What are you gonna do if this is where your mind is at?"

Clyde said, "My new song has to move forward. Because I feel like I'm changing."

"You're growing up. Fast, too."

"Whatever you call it. But I got to say something like, if we're looking for enemies, we will we always find one. *And* the computers and cameras will find so much bad stuff that we'll all be in trouble. But we'll also act like a judge. Throwing stones at each other back and forth. Who's gonna be left standing after all that?"

"Stupid-ass MARVIN," Nolan said.

"Heh, yeah. So that's where I'm at. I got some big ideas for this track. You feel me?"

"You're definitely ahead of the curve. Again! This one might vibe with even more folks."

"Yeah. You know," Clyde said, "I actually brought over some rough cuts of what I been workin' on. You maybe want to take a listen?"

"Of course!" Nolan said. "Better yet, we can put you in the new vocal booth and test it out. Come on, take a look."

They walked to a corner of the space where several long desks had been set up with computers, monitor speakers, and other hardware. Clyde ran over to a large enclosed structure and looked inside.

"Wow, Nolan! This is tight."

"A real game changer. I predict a lot of hits will

come out of there."

"Yeah? You already working with other artists?" Clyde asked quietly.

"Not yet, don't get all jealous. But I got so many ideas, even bigger than music or that news show. Like TV series, movies—all self-produced and self-financed. Complete creative control. Our message and our voice, with no middle man changing up what we got to say in order to make some *sheikh* dude happy."

"Who?"

Nolan said, "Foreign investors, man. The point is this—think about how many fingerprints that ain't black are all over projects that are supposedly FUBU."

"I don't know any of that, Nolan. You the man of the world. Tell me what's up."

"Picture a chess board right now."

"Okay," Clyde said.

"What do you see?"

"Bunch of white pieces and black pieces staring each other down."

"Right," Nolan said. "Now say it's the middle of the game. What's that look like?"

"They all tangled up. In the mix fighting. Some dead pieces sitting off to the side. And eventually, somebody gonna take the king and win."

"Alright, so that's chess in the controlled environment of a game. But in real life, most of the black pieces are pawns. Maybe only a few rooks and bishops in the mix. But ain't no kings or queens out there."

Clyde said, "Whatchu mean no queens? Every block around here, and at every club I been to around the country, sistas be walkin' around flaunting they stuff like they's queens."

Nolan let out a big laugh. "Oh, you funny, boy. I set

you right up for that one."

"Yup!" Clyde started singing, "Ebony princess, please say yes… Nubian queen, you are my dream!"

"There he go. Mr. Improv throwing away lines for free, like some baron giving out alms to the poor from his coach."

"Just sharing my gift with the world, haha," Clyde said with a laugh. "But, sorry. You were talking chess."

Nolan nodded. "Like I said, it's mostly pawns. And not only that, a lot of 'em *think* they're actually kings. That's the saddest thing I see around the hood, and it's what I try to teach all of y'all. Perspective. Even if you can't see everything, at least know where you at."

"True, true. So where am I at, then?"

"Hold on," Nolan said, "we'll get around to you later. I'm talking about *my* vision right now. The big plan! Hey, you ever hear of that TV show called *The Wire*?"

"I don't know," Clyde said.

"Anyway, real quick. Takes place in Baltimore about twenty-five years ago. And you know the score down there. But there's this guy named Stringer trying to get out of the drug business and go legit. So he hooks up with this corrupt brother who's a politician, thinking that's his ticket out and up. But nope! Politician played that man, even set him up for a cash drop using a white dude as bait."

"So," Clyde said, "he thought he was about to maybe become a knight, but he got fooled."

Nolan wagged a finger. "The pawn that wanted to be a black knight, ha! But you're wrong though—no one fooled him. He left himself exposed because he didn't gather all of the necessary information. Anyone can become a master of the level they're in, but then watch what happens when they try to move up. They just close their eyes, hoping and praying that it will all just happen for them. But that's not how they did it the first time. And why would anybody on the cruise ship let someone sitting in a rowboat get on board?"

Clyde said, "All these riddles, I don't know."

"They wouldn't! Unless you got something to offer."

"So how do we get on board?"

"Hell," Nolan said, "you already about on, kid genius. But it depends what you want to do on there. Think about the people with money who are chatting you up right now. Even though you busted out on your own, maybe they're just trying to fence you in as a reliable milk cow."

"Hmm. So that's why they're being so nice." Clyde paused. "A year ago, they would've seen right through me if I passed them on the street. Damn…"

Nolan said, "Don't get all sad about it, Jesus. You just got to be smart. That's what I've been saying. If you want to be a big player on the big stage on your own terms, you got to know how it all works."

"Man, I can't see that far ahead. This doesn't sound as fun as it used to be."

"Welcome to being a man! You already done provided for your moms and helped your sister out. Be proud about that, but also understand that success comes with responsibility if you want to maintain it. Look at my operation. I've been building it slowly for years, always reinforcing my gains brick by brick."

"So, what?" Clyde said. "Am I supposed to keep an eye on everything now? Not much time for creativity if I got to look at DJC like it's a store I'm running."

Nolan said, "But kid, that's your ticket to freedom! Being in charge of your own destiny, that's what it's all about."

"Nolan, this is too much to take in! Another one of your truth bombs dropped right on my head. Why don't you record these speeches and put them out on PerformTube instead?"

"And play by the rules on their boat?"

"How would you do it then?" Clyde asked.

"Build my own damn boat! That's what this whole place you're looking at right here is. I'll pull my own Stringer move, but with eyes open."

"Oh, okay. So I ain't alone in trying to do this."

"No, sir," Nolan said. "I'm standing right beside you on that chessboard. Now, shields up and swords out!"

Clyde grabbed a microphone stand and swung it through the air.

"Pawns," he said. "But not for long…"

14. THE SERMON

The Reverend Matthias G. Witherspoon was awake well before dawn. He arrived at his church in Akron, Ohio, just as the first hints of daylight began to peek through the clouds. The parishioners would start showing up in two hours for his Sunday sermon, and he could expect about an hour of solitude now before his support staff arrived.

Matthias first went into the annex which housed the Foundation for Healing Colonial Guilt, the outreach program he had established shortly after the HRA was born. It had been a good source of federal funds which, initially at least, were used to sponsor workshops that helped "build a bridge toward racial reconciliation."

But somewhere along the way, pride or vanity had led him, and in turn the foundation, very much astray. He had shamefully allowed the group leaders to go off script, by instead teaching the schoolchildren who had been bused in to feel either guilt or grievance, depending on their heritage. These workshops also drove a psychological wedge into the identities of mixed-race boys and girls who had the misfortune of attending.

Worst of all was his own behavior. For over a year, Reverend Witherspoon had been the ringleader whipping white men into a frenzy of contrition in debtors' prison yards across the region. What started out almost as a gag—"Let's see how far they'll let me take it"—grew into a traveling circus that had taken on a life of its own, with Matthias becoming just as enthralled by the power of his own voice as were the crowds he harangued.

The truth was that he had once been a thoughtful and reserved man, but always allowed himself to be led into temptation by his ego. On this morning in particular, he lamented that the name Witherspoon was considered a joke among serious people. Because during the month since the Sentinels of Jubilee first hacked into the HRA, Matthias grew more nauseous as it slowly dawned upon him that the program could actually be in jeopardy.

Even worse, he had to admit that like so many other black folk around the country, he hadn't taken what the HRA offered seriously enough, and instead let the weakest aspects of his personality run wild while the money flowed into his coffers.

Matthias left the church annex and entered the main building, then went into his private study. He pulled a stack of papers out of his briefcase and settled into his leather chair, putting on a pair of reading glasses as he reached for the desk lamp.

Here was the speech he intended to deliver in church today, one whose tone was much more serious than his usual theatrical fare. Because with an election only two days away, and so many people's fates hanging in the balance, the least he could do was try and rise to the occasion.

As he reviewed the sermon outline and made notes in the margins, Matthias sensed that certain points were not directly aimed at the congregation—or even the modest audience that would be watching live on the church's PerformTube channel—but possibly intended for one of his competitors, and almost as a plea for forgiveness.

Matthias closed his eyes. He was overcome with a feeling of juvenile envy as he pictured that eccentric man known only as the Prescient One. All this time, while Reverend Witherspoon was getting praise from regional press and being featured on European news programs, the world had scoffed at this weird new religion called Modestianity. Everyone thought that it was either a joke that would fizzle out, or a cult that would come to a bad end.

But now Matthias knew that people had it all backwards. While he himself had not been serious enough to seize the moment and use Reparations to bring his people across the finish line, his counterpart the Prescient One—who had been mocked and disrespected while steadily growing his church—it was *he* who had seen the crucial issue beyond the moment. And now he was the one offering a long-term vision to lead the nation out of its divisive squabbles, in order to face the bigger threat as voiced by the Sentinels.

The writing was on the wall now. Refugees were flocking to the Mall of Absolution while Matthias had done little of lasting impact to help his own community. The Mall was more than a place of shelter, because it also offered a fresh new vision for how to grapple with modern challenges.

But Matthias did not wish to upstage or defeat the Prescient One now. He simply wanted to be a worthy ally during this new War for Dignity, which he hoped would transcend the sputtering War for Equity. Because the cameras and microphones certainly didn't care what color your skin was or who your ancestors were. They were out there working nonstop, steadily compiling an impeccably thorough ledger on all people —and there was no telling when that bill would come due or how someone would be expected to pay it.

Today Reverend Witherspoon would take his shot at redemption in the only way he knew how—by using that silver tongue of his for good, and not merely to score points with bleeding hearts. But he could not do it alone, so he bowed his head and finally spoke to God as he was supposed to: in humility, and with no false fronts or evasions.

Matthias asked God to forgive him for wasting time and performing more for people's praise rather than His glory. He knew that there were countless ways in which he had chosen wrongly and therefore let his people down. But now he would let his own foibles fall away, so that he might finally share a message that was bigger than himself.

He understood that the fallout from this sermon might lead to being abandoned by his parishioners. If so, that would be fair recompense for what this fifty-four-year-old man had allowed himself to become. As he unclasped his hands, Matthias took heart in the notion that God buttresses those who act upon what they must do.

As the church bells tolled outside, Matthias left the study and walked out to his forest green Cadillac. He pulled a tin from the glove box and selected a piece of citrus hard candy, then took a moment to savor the textures and bitter flavor. With this calming ritual complete, the reverend was now ready to lead Sunday services.

"It is a blessed morning, my people, and I hope it finds you well. But the truth is, I greet you all with a heavy burden upon my heart. Still I give praise, because right now I've got the power of the Almighty God in my soul. While I am an imperfect vessel to deliver His word, I know that He will surely see me through.

"Exodus, fifteen: 'Thou in thy mercy hast led forth the people which thou hast redeemed: thou hast guided them in thy strength unto thy holy habitation.' Amen.

"Because the truth is that I messed up. A lot of us messed up. Too many of us didn't take Reparations for slavery seriously. And in the ultimate form of irony, it was all those white allies doing the heavy lifting to create the HRA—they *did* believe! But us? These past three, four years, we treated it like just another program to help catch a free ride.

"And we were wrong to behave like this. Because just like that, one little hack showed that it could go away in an instant. Now we have to hope that on Tuesday, we're granted four more years to prove we were worthy of Reparations after all. And if we get that chance, I hope we don't make the world regret it.

"Y'all need some tough love, though. We've got to start playing to our strengths, and stop deluding ourselves about our blind spots and shortcomings. Join with me in a little prayer of contrition. Pray with me now, as I thank the Lord Jesus Christ for His guidance out of my own prideful sins. I ask Him to give us all the strength to face that cruel mirror, so that we may be better and more truthful in our lives. I do solemnly swear that I will honor His teachings by loving my fellow man, both with praise when it is deserved, and correction when it is just.

"Oh, I see you fidgeting in your seats out there. Some of y'all don't like this new me. I get it. You want good-time Matthias to make you laugh. 'Haha, he a clown! It's the Sunday circus show!' But I can't do it no more. It's time to get serious, all of us, and start thinking about our futures for real. Picture that white-and-green HRA debit card in your purse, and imagine that it was gone forever. What would you do? How would you provide for your family?

"Oh Lord, I know they closed that factory down and sent it to China or Bangladesh or wherever. But a lot of Caucs lost their jobs when that happened, too. Yeah, I know they let in all those Mexicans who work on the cheap. But you know, they show up at the job site, stick around to raise their kids, and within one generation they're all dialed in. They speak English, finish high school, and can hold down a job.

"But what about us? Decade after decade, it's the same destructive cycle. Esther, chapter eight: 'For how can I endure to see the evil that shall come unto my people? Or how can I endure to see the destruction of my kindred?'

"You know what I think? I bet you that one day, maybe thirty years ago, the government just threw up their hands and gave up on us. Said something like, 'Let those Latizos in, see how they do.' And just like that, the Latizo population exploded. Give it another fifteen, twenty years, and think about how much political power they're gonna hold. And they ain't got none of that white guilt! No, sir! Are you starting to get it yet?

"That's why the time is *now* to make Reparations work. Somehow we got this last blessed chance at a hand up, and we must use it to get ourselves right instead of just punishing whites. Lord, I have been *so wrong* in playing that foolish game, and I ask that You forgive me. No, we have to turn that vengeful eye back onto ourselves and be held accountable, too.

"Because in reality, I have seen good white men in those debtors' prisons. And I know that when they're released, the home they go back to isn't some great mansion, neither. Plenty of poor Caucs killin' time down in the cell block, that's right!

"And the sad truth is, we get softer and weaker after every dollar we take from them. Meanwhile that Korean who owns your neighborhood convenience store, he's so disciplined that he can always squeeze out a profit—even while we steal from him. Because of course, we resent him. Proverbs, chapter twenty-one: 'The desire of the slothful killeth him; for his hands refuse to labor.'

"So I'm telling you now, the clock is running out. On patience. Money. Sorrow. And hope. We've got to stop complaining, stop gaming the system. Find some gratitude and turn it into pride. Say to the world, 'Yes, your ancestors sold me and your grandfathers shunned me. But today, you renew me so that tomorrow we can look forward together, unburdened by the weight of history that is crushing us all.'

"Look, my people. It's not hopeless. Progress has been made bit by bit since Barack Obama first knocked down that color barrier into the presidency twenty years ago. Yes, we're getting closer! But there's still so much shocking brutality within our own ranks. Crimes and killings done more out of callousness than desperation.

"Which is why I worry. I worry that one day, main street America is going to say that all the entertainment that college basketball provides, it's not enough to offset the endless cycle of single-motherhood by too-young teenage girls that produces more criminals than healthy members of society.

"Tell me, is the creative destruction within the black community really worth it? For every great singer who inspires the world, we leave a pile of black bodies in our wake. For every brilliant scholar, square miles of ruin. For every athlete that makes it big, how many others fall right back into the soup?

"Ezekiel, chapter five, verse fourteen: 'Moreover I will make thee waste, and a reproach among the nations that are round about thee, in the sight of all that pass by.' Because I swear it, the few eagles among us are not enough to sustain it all. I'm talkin' about the waste, the squandered potential, the unfulfilled dreams… We can't afford it no more! No one can.

"Especially when there's a whole world of people of *all* races out there who are eager to come take our place at the table. While we spill our glasses and throw food at each other, there are Africans, Russians, Filipinos, and Chinese standing outside the door politely. So is it any wonder that the system would rather import the Third World than deal with us? Before we call anyone racist, we better look in the mirror and ask why. Because they're already trying to phase us out!

"Don't hide your ears from my tough talk, I beg of you! These are just words, not bullets that kill. I'm pulling no punches today because if we don't get our act together in the next four years, we may be knocked down for the count.

"And then what are we gonna do? And where are we gonna go? Back to the Motherland, where we haven't stepped foot in centuries? Y'all couldn't survive in metal shacks or a mud hut. You've never even been camping! But I'm with you on that. I like my shower too much. So we can't go back! We've got to make the most of what we have right here. And I quote Psalm Thirty-three, 'Blessed is the nation whose God is the

Lord; and the people whom he hath chosen for his own inheritance.'

"So let's start by showing a little respect. 'For what?' that lady just said. For what?! Hahaha! For the food, the shelter, the cars, the electricity, and the roads. For the cell phone you use to call your sister and listen to your favorite songs—and which you *could* use to better yourself, like learning a new language instead of looking at pornography.

"All these tools are at your disposal, but the choice what to do with them is still up to you. Your ancestors would have *killed* for something that offered a person —any man, woman, or child—access to a way out of ignorance. Oh Lord, you can lead a horse to water, but you can't make him drink. And you can give an Afrigro-American the key to his enlightenment, but you can't make him think.

"That is, unless he wants to! So, do you? Do you, my brothers and sisters, want to make the best of your mind in this wonderful country to improve your own lot in life? Because I can't do it for you. The Caucs can't do it for you. And most definitely, that magic money coming from the Historical Reparations Administration isn't the cure. Otherwise people who win the lottery wouldn't end up so miserable and broke once again. That's right! I am preaching truth right now! Stand back!

"Say, you, Mr. Morris. How much money you got on you right now? Eleven dollars? Tell me, how much has the HRA paid you and what have you done with it? Did you use it to better your life, or did you waste it? *What did you spend it on?!*

"All that money, which they say was earned by the blood and sweat and tears of our ancestors. And yet you used it to get drunk on cognac, thinkin' you was a prince. Don't tell me y'all haven't seen the costs go up on our favorite vices now. Because you know they have —but every day, you still pull out that debit card and let them swipe away the gift that was paid for in pain.

"Or maybe you like to gamble. I see the hustles you boys run in the doorways of those vacant shops. Losing money you should be investing to open new businesses in those same storefronts. It's so easy, too. All you'd have to do is show the smallest bit of initiative and it could be yours. Why? Because the color of your skin will get you in! Yes indeed! Say it with me now. The color of your skin… will get you in!

"You got to plan out the next step. Because I'm tellin' you right now, equity isn't enough. That's right, it ain't! You know that old 'teach a man how to fish' line? Well, I think it's missing something. Because it's not just about putting food on a black man's plate, or his ability to grow crops of his own. What we need is to be able to *participate* in the future! Don't you want to be involved in that struggle to move humanity forward, rather than just playing dominoes in the park?

"Do not let this opportunity slip away. Oh my Lord, if Victor Dominguez wins do you not think that the Latizo population won't flex its muscles and say no more? My God Almighty, did you just hear me? If Dominguez wins, that might be the end of any kind of sympathy for our godforsaken race. Not when there's Mexicans and Koreans and Indians here by the millions and two generations deep.

"And they don't feel the slightest twitch of guilt. No sir, they are not weighed down by the white man's albatross. But go on, keep it up. Keep playing the fool and testing their patience. Just remember, the 'new Americans' are moving forward day by day.

" 'But Reverend,' you say. 'Them foreigners ain't suffered like our people.' Oh yeah? You don't know that. You would, if you bothered to use your tablet to read about world history and not play video games. Did you know that there was a war in Korea seventy-five years ago that split their proud nation in half? That's where North Korea and South Korea come from. Yes, 'the North and the South.' Hmm, where have we heard that before? That's right, Koreans had their own civil war.

"And then there's India, my god! If you saw the poverty over there—the filth, the desperation!—you'd get up off your hind ends so fast and never complain again. But no, you just want to stay in your little bubble where the narrative says that you can take, but not give. Use, but not create.

"So answer me this. If the narrative you believe also says that our African ancestors built up this nation from nothing without fair pay, will you just stand around while people who got here last week take over? 'Cause they're coming. They'll sweep your craps game off the stoop and move their whole family in, then start selling you junk to pay for their kids' college. And in twenty years they'll be gone, moved out to the nice neighborhoods where none of y'all live. You know and I know that when that happens, they won't even bother to say thank you for using us as their stepping stones to the American Dream.

"My people, I know that my words today are harsh and shocking. But this is a wake up call! As I turn over a new page in my own life and seek to become a more serious man, I extend my hand so that you all will join me. Do as I do from now on. Respect yourself and be the best men and women that you can be, because maybe the narrative *is* correct when we cry out that ain't no one coming to help us.

"We've got to start working together to create our own wealth. Effective tomorrow, I will begin reorganizing the Foundation for Healing Colonial Guilt to help facilitate entrepreneurship among members of this congregation and our community at large.

"So yes, after wading through all that muck, I hope to end this sermon on a positive note. Deep in my heart, I have tremendous hope for all of us, because I know that the story isn't over. That our history of suffering is only part of the whole. It is, in fact, the part that precedes our redemption and fulfillment in this great land of opportunity.

"And that is why, despite it all, we are glad to be here and not back in Africa. Because our painful journey through history bought us advance tickets in getting to know our Lord Jesus Christ. At this very moment, there are millions and millions of our cousins over there who never heard His name or learned His gospel. Hundreds of years of black men and women who the slave traders *didn't* catch, but who also lived and died in complete ignorance of the true God.

"Stand up and raise your hands for me now, because I can't do this alone. God is responsible for every gift and every tribulation. He's at your side during every glorious moment and bears witness to every tragic scene. The good and the bad are what it means to be human! No one goes through this life unscarred, and no one gets out alive. So don't hold yourselves back just because of grief or imperfection, not when you've got the power of Jesus Christ alive in your heart and in your mind!

"That is *your* privilege. A glorious strength that billions of people of all races around the world do not possess. Honor it and honor Him by leaving here today with a newfound sense of appreciation for what you have, and a reaffirmed faith that He has a wonderful plan for you.

"May God bless you all. Amen..."

15. ELECTION EVE

Victor Dominguez and his wife Jaclyn were alone at home in Scottsdale. They had flown in earlier after last-minute appearances in Michigan, where his team believed that poll numbers suggested the state was suddenly in play.

Jaclyn brought a tray into the living room and placed a scotch-on-the-rocks on the table beside Victor's recliner.

"Thank you."

"My pleasure. It's so nice to have a few minutes to ourselves after all this time flying around."

"Are you ready to be the first lady of our nation?"

Jaclyn sat down and said, "I've been with you every step of the way so far. Count me in."

Victor turned to the iguana that was lounging on the arm of his chair. "And what about you, Tito? Do you have what it takes to be the first pet?"

The iguana flicked its tongue. Victor gave him a gentle squeeze on the ribs.

"I wonder what the kids will think if I bring him to

the Easter Egg Roll."

"You know, Victor. One day when I'm old and frail, in my last memoirs I think I'll finally reveal that Tito was your most trusted sounding board when you had to make the tough decisions."

"As long as it's the right choice, the methods don't matter."

"Then I hope he survives the next four years."

"Or eight."

"One step at a time, darling."

"So, which one of you should I kill first?" Ryan Richards said with villainous contempt.

His head lay across his arm and he was staring at a row of shots set out on the bar. Some were clear, others brown, and still others golden. Suddenly he perked up.

"I know! Let's go with the buddy system."

He lifted two of the glasses to his lips, then tilted them back sloppily. As Ryan wiped his face with his sleeve, a silver-haired real estate tycoon with a spray tan that rivaled his own sat on the stool next to him.

"Why are you so down in the dumps?"

"I just have a bad feeling about the election," Ryan said. "My job's on the line too."

"There's no way she's going to lose. Look at everybody else here. They're relaxing, having a good time. It's in the bag. Everyone knows it but you."

The tycoon reached over and picked up one of the shot glasses.

"Help yourself," Ryan chuckled. "I want to believe you. I'm just so wrapped up in it, you know? I don't have any perspective right now."

"What's the big problem, anyway? Every acting gig you ever had came to an end at some point. Don't tell me you didn't save up enough money?"

"I've got plenty of cash in the bank. And my DS isn't even all that bad considering how long my family's been here. But if Jeffries-Lao goes down and *DDM* gets canceled, or if they decide to go in another direction with a new host…"

"You're giving yourself an ulcer over nothing."

"Did you know that after *Antiques Roadshow* got canceled, the producers didn't just get blacklisted from the industry? They went into hiding! So if the pendulum swings back the other way, I don't know if I have enough in the tank to reinvent myself again. If they even let me."

The other man laughed. "What's it been since you last played Rolph Dungeonlord? Eight years?"

"Something like that. Don't remind me, please."

"Why? He was fun! Maybe bring him back, start swinging that battle-ax around again. You know, for nostalgia's sake."

"Christ… Will that be my only option if this all falls apart? I forgot most of my German anyway."

"Ryan, let me put this in perspective for you. If Dominguez wins and they start dismantling the HRA, we're all gonna have more to worry about than who gets cast as what on TV."

Richards straightened up. "I'll be damned. You're right. It will be," he called out dramatically while lifting a glass, "a time of change!"

"That's the spirit. Now bottoms up."

"Let us eat and drink, for tomorrow we die!"

Glenn Murray whipped his head around like a windmill and pumped his fist. The guitar player to his left flashed his teeth menacingly while strumming with blinding speed. The mosh pit in front of the stage swirled in rhythm to the kick-drum's punchy beat, and the smell of sweat and beer filled this small Providence bar.

"Fury!" Glenn howled into the microphone that was cupped in his hand. "Furious at the lies! In front, behind, coming from all sides. Behold the corruption if you dare, then fall to your knees, escape is nowhere…"

"Crisis actors are a girl's best friend!"

Eileen Jeffries-Lao slid back over the arm of a soft lounge chair and kicked off her heels. Paul Jeffries caressed one of her stockinged feet as he walked past and sat in a matching chair. He set two drinks down on the coffee table, then loosened his tie.

"Well," he said, "I just hope the detaining officers haven't abused him too badly."

"I'm sure their supervisor was briefed that no harm should come to our 'suspect'. Otherwise, hazard pay!" Eileen reached out from her awkward position and scooted a glass into her fingers. "But it's fine. Our little ruse has already paid dividends."

"Oh, really?"

"Yes, indeed! Someone who works for the HRA in Dallas turned herself in."

"A woman? Hmm."

"She's fairly low level, but has been dating one of the IT guys who works at the same location. Apparently he 'turned' her to the dark side. But seeing all the panic at her branch firsthand, and then sensing that our nets were closing in—it gave her a change of heart."

"And the boyfriend?"

"Ah. We picked him up during his lunch break yesterday. And he's been singing ever since! Now the poor fellow won't be able to cast his vote for Dominguez tomorrow."

Paul leaned forward and tipped an imaginary hat. "Finally, a crack in the dam. That's great news!"

"And he's not the only one."

"Really now?"

"I wish we could've done it sooner for PR's sake, but the point is we'll now be sweeping up some of the top Jubileers."

"Anyone I might know?"

Eileen shrugged her shoulders. "National security. Sorry, hon."

"I do wish you wouldn't keep so many secrets from me. I hate to put my foot in my mouth when being interviewed."

"I know, it's a tough gig having to toe that fine line between platitudes and evasions."

"Despite your own little evasion here, congratulations nonetheless."

"Thank you, Paul. I don't think my team was too happy about us staging an arrest five days before the election, but it gave me a nice boost in the polls, and now—"

"Now they can focus on taking down the Sentinels in time for you to make a rousing inaugural speech."

"Oh, Mr. Jeffries, you have such a knack for dramatic timing."

"Please. The first man *does* do more than drink bourbon and hobnob with dignitaries."

"You won't mind such a taxing workload for another four years, will you?"

"As long as there's still time to keep my golf swing in rhythm, I'm the man for the job."

"Well… We all have our vices."

Ms. Jenkins came in from the garage with a hamper under her arm. She stopped when she saw that Myra was standing at the front window looking out into the street.

"I don't think he's coming back tonight," she said. "Get away from there and help me with these clothes."

Myra slowly pushed through the canvas drapes and walked toward the dining room table. She picked up a shirt, saying as she began to fold it, "I just don't understand why. Everything, and I mean everything, has been going so good for us all."

Ms. Jenkins balled up a tiny pair of yellow socks. "He been a wild, strong man for a long time. Made the best of himself considering where he started. Song or no song, it got to be hard for him to come into our house. Be dealin' with women and babies, when out there on the streets he got excitement and... the unknown."

"Oh, Mama. He's been so good with Sarah lately, too. Buying her gifts, singing her little songs. I just don't know how he can switch that off so quick."

"I guess he still ain't decided whether he wants to be part of this family, or..."

"Or what? Keep chasing after other girls?"

"That ain't the all of it. Sometimes men, they just get stuck in this mode, like they's lone wolves roaming in the night. So lost, they don't even realize when they got what they was after."

"So what do I do?"

"About Octavius? Nothing. You take care of you and these kids. Better to have him 'round here only if he want to be."

Myra glanced at Sarah bouncing lazily in her swing. She bunched her lips and kept folding clothes.

Upstairs Tyrell was watching an animated TV show. Two squirrels in red spacesuits teleported into a hall filled with purple entities that were shaped like tall floor lamps. The visitors were greeted by the flashing on and off of their bulbous heads.

One of the squirrels said, "Salutations from Earth! We are grateful for this welcome, but are troubled by all of the energy expended in such a display. Remember: conserve resources, save the planet!"

A purple character waddled forward. "We do not receive many visitors on our remote world. Those that do come are usually pleased with our hospitality. Who are you to take offense?"

"We are the Impact Kids! Traveling into the deepest reaches of space to share our wisdom—efficiency, utility, coopera…"

Tyrell turned his attention away from the TV to his tablet. It was much nicer than the ones he and his classmates used at school. He spent a lot of time exploring all the interactive learning games which his uncle Clyde had installed on it.

But tonight Tyrell wasn't playing one of those. He entered the DoWork program and opened a file called *home*. A spreadsheet appeared and he scrolled down until reaching a cell with the words *week three*.

He selected a box next to the one labeled *mommy* and typed, "said a bad word 5 times. didnt flush last nite". Tyrell then moved to a line designated for his grandmother and entered, "yell at the mail man…"

He glanced up at the TV screen. The two astrosquirrels were standing in front of a commander back on their ship. They turned to the camera and said, "Join us next time as we nobly scurry where no bushy tail has scurried before!"

Octavius was sitting in his Buick. His right hand gripped the top of the steering wheel, but the engine was off. Searing yellow from a nearby streetlight reflected off his dark face.

He looked around—empty parking lot, couple of closed stores, quiet street, then a row of houses. Nothing going down at the moment, but he knew that around here that could change in an instant. So you always had to be ready, because instigator or not, it was on you to survive.

He was twenty-eight years old. Already a veteran of the street life. But all this family business, first with Myra and especially now that Clyde was involved, was getting him confused. His daughter was turning into a beautiful little girl. And this goofy kid Clyde wanted him along for the ride with his music career.

It was all too warm and gray for someone like himself who lived in a world of absolutes, where you had to stay detached if you didn't want to be the next victim. But the life was a grind, constantly looking over your shoulder and having to put on displays of confidence. Buying souped-up cars and fancy matching jewelry, not because you wanted those things, but because that kind of flair commanded respect. And out here, that could save your life.

Octavius figured that sooner or later it was all going to catch up with him. Hustle for long enough and it didn't matter how you looked or who you were in good with. Someone new was always gunning for your corner.

To think that hooking up with Clyde, at the cost of putting him out of his comfort zone, might give him a way to walk out of here on his own two feet, instead of leaving in a body bag…

Well, he thought, *there's worse ways to go.*

Octavius turned the ignition and pulled into the street. He could already picture Sarah's little eyes smiling at him from her crib.

Eddie Pryor closed his eyes and draped an arm over the microphone stand. He nodded his head to the rhythm of the song before doing his best Wayne Newton impression.

"The love between the two of us was dying…"

When the song finished he peacocked over to three Vietnamese women in matching lavender dresses. They devoured him as he fell into their booth.

"Girls, girls," he said as he sat up, "it is damn good to be alive!"

The trio laughed and tried to smooth his hair and shirt collar.

"So," Eddie said, "which one of you is gonna go up there and serenade me?"

"Oh, no, no!" they laughed. "We don't sing."

"How the hell am I supposed to make you ladies famous if you won't even go up in front of a bowling alley crowd?"

"Famous, who?" one of the girls said. "We want to have fun."

"Yeah? Are you having fun? Good, good."

"Oh, very much fun! And even if we don't sing, maybe later we dance for you."

Eddie waved over the server. "Get these dolls whatever they want. And another whiskey soda for me —if I'm gonna do all the singing for this group, I need to keep these pipes lubricated. Whoo!"

Elder Marcus Young was making his final evening rounds before settling in for the night. The Mall's weekly publication had just come out and he wanted to read the latest news.

He looked in on a resident who had arrived with bronchitis. A nurse was making notes in her tablet while the man slept.

"How is he coming along?" Marcus said.

The nurse nodded her head slightly. "We got the coughing under control."

"That's a good sign."

"But he's in rough shape. Malnourished. Frail. Addressing these symptoms is just the first step."

"Thank you, nurse." Marcus turned to leave.

"And how about you, sir?"

"Doing fine. Thank you for asking. I think the first couple of days were hectic for everyone, but now we're all settling in."

"If there's anything you need," she said, "don't hesitate to ask. The staff here has seen it all—inner city ERs, meth country, you name it—so you can rely on us."

"Wonderful. Have a modest evening."

Marcus clasped his hands behind his back and walked softly down the hallway toward the front of the building. He kept his ears alert for any sound that might indicate one of the patients was in distress.

As he passed the sliding double doors that led into the entertainment room, he saw that several of the men were playing cards. He approached them with a wave.

One of the men grumbled and threw his cards onto the table. James Haggerston reached out and gathered up the pot, saying, "Mmm, mmm, mmm."

Bo also flicked his cards away and cursed. He glanced over at Marcus.

"Hey, boss. What's the word?"

Marcus stepped closer. "Good evening, gents. I was just taking a last look around before retiring. Is everything well with you?"

"Yeah. It would go better if James didn't win so many hands."

James threw his hands up. "Is it my fault these guys don't know how to bluff?"

Marcus stepped back, saying, "I'll leave you to your sordid ways, then."

"Say," Bo called out, "you want to sit in, play a few hands?"

"Oh, I don't know. This is your thing."

"Come on, man! You can't just play nanny all the time. Come hang out with us."

Marcus gave a sly smile. "Alright. Just remember, back before I found Mod, I was pretty worldly. I don't want to hear any crying if I take all your money."

"This guy!" Bo said. "Now he's a card shark."

"I wash my hands of it. Deal!"

Luis Ortega was studying at the kitchen table. His mother dried her hands and shuffled past into the living room. She sat down next to her husband, who was watching soccer on the TV.

A few minutes later, the sound of voices close by came in through the open front windows. Mrs. Ortega got up and looked outside.

"*Dios,*" she sighed as she pulled back.

"*Que pasa?*" Mr. Ortega asked.

"There are people outside in the driveway. Young people."

"Luis's *amigos*, no?"

"*Yo no se.* Excuse me, Luis? I think some of your

friends from the school are here."

Luis looked up from his work. "I don't know, Mama. We usually meet in the library on campus."

"Can you please go and check who they are?"

Luis got up and stepped out onto the front stoop. There were about twenty people standing together, and several held lighted candles with religious figures printed on the glassware.

"Ahhh," the group said when they saw him.

Luis adjusted his glasses. "Hey, can I help you guys?"

"Oh, Luis," they began to sing, "sweet Luis. A boy so brave, they fell to their knees…"

Luis brought a hand to his forehead, then waved at the group until they stopped singing. "Who are you, anyway?"

A man in his mid-twenties stepped forward. "We are," he said proudly, "Luis's Lieutenants. And we are here to serve!"

"Wait… What the hell?"

"Everyday people with busy lives, just like you. And thanks to your courageous example, we all found each other."

"But how'd you guys find my house?" Luis asked. "I mean, like, did you just come over to say hi?"

A young Latiza around Luis's age emerged from the group.

"This is Cristina," the man said. "Go on, tell him."

The girl looked down. "I got a DDM notification a few days ago. But I'm on a gymnastics travel team—I don't wanna go!"

"But it should be fine," Luis said. "They told me Beneficiaries can put it off til later if they want."

"That's the thing," she said. "Inside I'm mostly white. The show called me on as a Debtor! Saint Luis, can you help me, please?"

She ran forward and hugged him. At first Luis stepped back to get away, but when she looked up he could see her face clearly in the light. He thought she was really cute.

"I don't know," he said, easing out of her arms. "But maybe we can think of something."

"Thank you," she whispered.

The group linked arms and started to sway back and forth. "Oh, Luis… Sweet Luis…"

Emissary Karlov entered the Prescient One's private chambers and saw that the thicket of blue cloth vines had been opened up by tying them off into neat bunches. He walked across the space and found his leader sitting tensely on the edge of a divan.

The Prescient One rose and said, "So good of you to join me, Emissary Karlov."

"But of course," Karlov said. "I would be remiss to decline such an invitation. How can I be of service?"

"Please, sit down. You have always offered me valuable help in the past when I was troubled—even if it was just lending me your ear. So please, indulge me now once more."

Karlov settled into a plush chair. "It would be an honor. What concerns you tonight?"

The Prescient One said, "As we speak most of the country, if not the world, is nervously awaiting the results of tomorrow's election. But of course, the scope of our upcoming expansion is so vast that political matters are almost inconsequential."

"Indeed," the emissary said. "The church is channeling your prescient insights so that we may be humble leaders and not merely followers—or even reactionaries, if you can pardon my frankness."

"I adore you for it," the Prescient One said with a mild laugh. "And that is why I asked you to join me. As we prepare to move forward with these bold steps, I find myself experiencing ripples of doubt. But whether it is simply about the church or perhaps something deeper within myself, I cannot tell."

"I see," Karlov said. "Forgive if what I'm about to suggest risks overstepping my bounds, but I only mean well. Shall I continue?"

"By all means."

"No one here, least of all me, doubts your sincerity or the rightness of your vision. But perhaps the outward manifestation of your push for modesty belies... something more personal about you. The old you, in fact."

The Prescient One touched a piece of putty that was stuck to his cheek, then yanked it off. "Do you refer to this? That perhaps Mod could have been shared with the world a bit... differently?"

Karlov said, "Far be it from me to question methods which, however unorthodox, have resonated with so many people. Modestianity has saved thousands from being held hostage to shame, and in turn given their lives a grounded sense of pride. But if you are afflicted with doubts at this critical juncture, surely they must not be ignored. If something destructive has been hiding deep within your subconscious, perhaps since long before your first major success twenty years ago —well, you must face it down right now!"

"Something going that far back in time, you think?" the Prescient One asked. "And it may have played a hand in the eccentricities that accompanied my philosophy right from the start? I don't even know whether it is benevolent, malevolent, or benign. How might I go about discovering the truth, Emissary?"

"There is only one way," Karlov said. "You must open yourself up to Mod more than you ever have before. Only by becoming truly vulnerable will He guide you to the deepest wounds."

"I see. Take off the *inner* mask."

"Yes, Your Prescience."

The Prescient One opened his mouth as if to speak, but then hesitated. A moment later he said, "But what if at the end of this process, I no longer believe?"

"In Mod?" Karlov asked.

"In Him, the church, all of it. Because if I don't know who has lurked within me for all these years, how can I be certain that after looking him in the eye, any of who I am today will survive?"

Karlov made a circular motion around his chest. "I offer my sincere prayers that this does not happen. But in that worst case, the church will carry on your mission. I swear it."

"Beloved Emissary," the Prescient One said, "I know you will. But what if the new me declares itself your mortal enemy?"

The emissary said, "Your words make me shiver. I know very little about your past private life. I pray that we all have not been misled by a man who secretly harbored a devil inside."

"And I as well. I regret if our conversation has shaken you so. That was not my intention."

"And yet only a few moments ago, it was I who feared offending you. Still, I am an emissary with good reason. Delve well, Your Prescience, and I shall greet whichever version of you returns."

"Thank you for this frank discussion. I beg Mod to shine upon us all."

TJ and David walked across the movie theater lobby and stepped into the concessions line.

"This was such a great idea to get out of the house," TJ said.

"I know!" David said. "There's only so much of those talking heads you can take."

"And there'll be *no* talking at all tonight, haha."

"I can't believe we're going to see a movie that's over a hundred years old on the big screen."

"Who needs 3D anyway?"

"Well," David said as he grabbed hold of TJ's arm, "we've got it where it really counts."

"Thanks for always being there, my love. Now, let's pick out some snacks…"

Dramacrat Congresshuman Neil Thornton sat typing frantically at the work desk in his country house. After sending each email, he also crossed one line off the list of gibberish words that ran down a piece of paper.

When he was done, he burned the sheet with a match. Then he took the computer into the kitchen and put it the microwave. Sparks and crackles gave way to a cloud of noxious smoke. Neil covered his face with the neck of his sweater, popped the microwave door open, then sprayed a fire extinguisher inside.

After cleaning himself up, he opened a beer and poured some Scotch into a tumbler, then returned to his desk. He slid the drawer open and removed a silver revolver. He checked the chamber—all six rounds were there—then pushed it back into place. He set the gun down and took a sip of beer as he relaxed into the high-backed leather chair.

A violent crashing sound of glass breaking came from behind him. Several dull pops followed. The air hissed and began to fill with smoke. Thin beams of red light strobed through the room as gruff male voices shouted to each other.

Congresshuman Thornton leaned forward and placed his hands face down on the surface of the desk. The unified force of three SWAT members wrenched him out of the chair and into the cold night air. A dozen officers formed a circle around him, while two S'more Stoppers buzzed loudly overhead.

As he was being cuffed, the team leader approached and said, "Looks like the Sentinels' days are numbered."

"Watch," Neil said with a grin, "I'll still keep my seat tomorrow."

"Take him away…"

"… So everybody, please put your hands together for the man behind this uniquely American story of inspiration, Mr. Nolan Simmons!"

Nolan jogged up and shook the host's hand. The audience gave warm applause as he took the podium.

"I'd like to thank the New Haven Optimist Club for inviting me to speak tonight. As if my life hadn't already been a fascinating journey, these past few months have taken it to a whole new level.

"But I speak from the heart when I say that nothing gives me greater pleasure than being able to share my insights with respected institutions like this one. Let's have a real conversation about how to improve communities and put powerful new ideas into action.

"Surely by working together, we can raise up the millions of Americans of all races who may be down and out right now, but are just looking for that opportunity to shine. I truly believe that most people want that feeling of pride that comes from contributing to their communities.

"Tonight I will discuss the main points of my new program, Nolan's Nine Strategies to Navigating Success…"

Kate and Chris Donohugh were at home glued to the TV. The various food containers strewn about were proof of their commitment to finishing all the leftovers that were in the fridge.

But conversation was sparse, and it was only the frantic election prognosticators on screen whose voices filled the air. A segment ended and the channel cut to commercial. Kate's face appeared.

"Oh, God," Kate moaned and fell forward onto a pillow.

"Come on," Chris said, "you have to watch."

"Fine, alright."

The Kate on TV said, "I'm Kate Donohugh, HRA employee and lifelong advocate. Our opponents will stop at nothing to try and tear us down. And while I may be one of their victims, let's make sure it doesn't happen ever again. On Tuesday, cast your vote for strong leadership by re-electing President Eileen Jeffries-Lao."

The commercial then cut to a wide shot of Kate and the president standing side by side.

"Make no mistake," Jeffries-Lao said. "I take these hackers and their fear tactics very seriously. Send me back to Washington so that I can stand up for Kate, fight for Beneficiaries, and keep our proud nation moving forward."

Chris clapped his hands and called out, "Bravo, bravo! Encore, please!"

Kate lowered the TV volume. "I hope that helps, but jeez, I hate to watch myself."

"I thought you looked kind of hot in that business suit. Can you model it for me?"

"Hey, what's got into you?" she said. "All week you've been in shutdown mode."

"Come on, it's not like you're Miss Consistent either. I mean, that message you left me is still standing here like the elephant in the room."

Kate sighed. "I don't know. I just feel like we haven't been on the same page for a while."

"Maybe some of it's just life happening. But you *are* the one who chose to travel around and then stay with your parents. You barely talked to me the whole time."

"I was feeling pretty lost. I just needed a breather."

"How'd that work out for you?" Chris scoffed.

"Why are you being so testy?"

Chris put his hands on the top of his head. He said, "All this stuff that's been going on has me really confused. And I guess it's dragging me down. I mean, if you had come back from that meeting with the president and said you'd accepted a job working for her down in DC—that I could maybe understand. But wanting to have a baby? That's the last thing I imagined you'd ever say."

"But it wasn't just from talking to her," Kate said. "It's everything that's happened this month. This year, really. Facing my own mortality. And seeing my old teacher, Ms. Herron. She *inspired* us back when we were in high school—but now she just seems like a witch casting spells. Oh my god, I can't believe I even said that."

"She's irrelevant, you don't really mean it."

"No, I mean how it reflects back on me. All of us. It's as if every classroom has its own pied piper luring children away from their parents, from their own desires—from whatever they'd known to be true before entering that school building."

"Kate," Chris said, "do you actually think teachers have the power to unravel kids' minds and reshape them just like that?"

"When you give them ten years to work on you, maybe!"

"If that's all true," Chris said slowly, "what I want to know is this. Who gave them the right to access our minds?"

"More like," Kate said, "why did they *think* they had that authority? We were innocent children!"

"What does that say about our educational system?"

"What does that say about us? We're products of that system. We've been doing its bidding out in the world for a long time."

Chris said, "So if you were brainwashed, then wasn't I too?"

"I… What would that mean to you, Chris?"

"I have to wonder then, how did it change the course of my own life? I mean, what if I didn't join a political band back when I started playing guitar, but spent that time learning classical or jazz? Maybe I could've become a great musician…"

"This is all getting too crazy," Kate said. "I don't know how much deeper I can go right now. Especially if you're in the water without a life jacket too!"

"Alright, Kate. Let's just rest. Have some calm before the storm tomorrow."

"I agree. And we really should make time for a day date soon. Go to brunch, maybe see a movie afterward.

Just have some fun together."

"Sign me up," Chris said.

"God, I hope she wins." Kate shook her head. "I don't know if I have the strength to face the alternative."

"We'll do the best we can, no matter what."

"I do love you, Chris."

"I know, babe."

The woman dipped the mop head into the water, then rolled the bucket forward by holding onto the handle as she walked. She gave the wringer a firm press, then made several precise strokes across the vinyl floor.

She worked her way down the corridor steadily. After reaching a turn, she called out, "Stepping into ladies room!"

The woman entered the restroom without the cleaning supplies. She bent over a sink and rinsed her face, then retied the strands of brunette hair that had come loose while working. She stood up and looked into the mirror—the bright-green-and-white striped jumpsuit and her tired eyes reflected back.

She saw one of the stall doors behind her slowly swing open. She whipped around to see a man staring at her. Before she could even gasp, let alone scream, he leaped out and grabbed hold of her. He looked intently into her eyes, until finally her shock gave way to recognition.

"Oh, Morgan," she moaned in a whisper. She threw her arms around him and sobbed into his chest.

"Emily, I'm here," he said quietly. "I can't stay long. Are you alright?"

The woman pulled back and wiped her eyes. "It's

awful. After work they make us come to this clinic and clean up all the messes."

"And the kids—where are our kids?"

"I still don't know anything!" she said more loudly, then quickly covered her mouth. "They just took them away after we got arrested. No one's told me anything since you all escaped. Now… God, I missed you so much!"

Morgan looked down at his watch. "I have to go. The guys who got me in here are waiting outside. I just had to see you, had to let you know I'm out there trying to make things right. One day we'll all be a family again."

Emily put her hand on his cheek. "Find them. No matter what it takes. Just find our children and bring them back to me."

"I swear to God, I will."

A moment later, the ladies room door opened and the woman in green stripes took up her mop. She kept her head down as she worked, so that the security cameras would not see her tears.

Clyde Jenkins sat writing lyrics at a dining table in the little furnished apartment he had rented. It was a safe haven for when things got too crazy, and this was just one of those times he needed to be alone. Everyone was talking about the election, asking him what he thought was going to happen with the HRA—but his head was somewhere else.

His thoughts went back to the summer, to the moment right before he sent his first song into that great content pipeline where unknown artists vied for a place in the zeitgeist. He'd felt like a little boy running along the sidewalks, oblivious to the workings of the world that made the buildings he passed possible, or how the businesses inside them operated.

But somehow, now millions of people knew his name and could recite his lyrics. Were they fools? As much as he enjoyed being showered with praise, Clyde was uneasy about being called a prophet or a revolutionary. He may have stumbled into the cultural conversation because of some unfathomable stroke of good timing, but he knew it wouldn't happen like that the second time around.

Clyde made his peace with the decision to go forward with the new song as-is, because even though the message was different, it came from the same place as before—his heart. So whether the response was a rocket launch even higher or an echo that never returned, what mattered was knowing that he'd followed his own instincts in the face of temptation.

Whenever he felt too stressed, he reminded himself that he was already playing with house money. He had taken the steps to provide for his family, first and foremost. And the words that had made him famous were not superficial, but actually gave other Beneficiaries insight into their own lives—as well as spread a little hope that things might improve at the HRA.

Sometimes the little boy inside him whispered that he was too young and uneducated to understand all of the HRA's inner workings, so who was he to criticize? All Clyde could do in the face of such doubts, was to put his trust in the poet's ability to cut through the world's complex structures and grasp the core ideas holistically.

And right now, Clyde felt that everybody needed to rein in their frantic thoughts and just be in the moment. They would do better to look inside for strength, and not elsewhere for help. Most of all, he wanted people to reach a hand across the street, instead of overwhelming themselves by trying to change the whole world.

Sometimes it was your own small efforts, made sincerely and without expectations, that ended up reverberating far and wide. Not because you shouted, but because other people spoke your name.

Clyde Jenkins, the unlikely hip-hop sensation, was ready to try his luck once more.

THE END.

BUT THE STORY CONTINUES IN…

REPARATIONS CORE

& REPARATIONS MAZE.

ABOUT THE AUTHOR

Originally from Northern Virginia, Philip Wyeth has lived in the Los Angeles area for many years. He's an entrepreneur, musician, film aficionado, hockey fan, and enjoys playing tennis and golf.

Inspired by such unique writers as Heinrich von Kleist, Ambrose Bierce, Joseph Conrad, and Len Deighton, Wyeth's imaginative novels will resonate with fans of Philip K. Dick, Rich Larson, Michel Houellebecq, and Neal Stephenson.

Also a lifelong fan of heavy metal music and its many sub-genres, Wyeth strives to infuse his writing with comparable levels of intensity, independence, and larger-than-life visions.

His website is www.philipwyeth.com, and you can follow him across the social media landscape under the following handles:

@PhilipWyeth: Twitter, BitChute, Gab, and Minds.

@PhilipWyethWriter: Instagram and Facebook.